His Brother's Bride

Canadian Historical Brides Book2
Ontario

By Nancy M Bell

Amazon Print 9781772994971

Books We Love
A quality publisher of genre fiction.
Airdrie Alberta

D1274975

Dedication

Books We Love Ltd. dedicates the Canadian Historical Brides series to the immigrants, male and female who left their homes and families, crossed oceans and endured unimaginable hardships in order to settle the Canadian wilderness and build new lives in a rough and untamed country.

For those who lost their lives in the Great War and for those who survived without them.

Lest We Forget

Acknowledgement

Books We Love acknowledges the Government of Canada and the Canada Book Fund for its financial support in creating the Canadian Historical Brides series.

Funded by the Government of Canada | Canada

Chapter One

Annie Baldwin pushed the wide brimmed bonnet up off her forehead and wiped the moisture with a fold of her long skirt. Haying was better than digging potatoes in the fall or hoeing rows in the garden, she supposed. But why was it always so hot and humid when it was time to mow the meadow?

"Annie, get a move on!" Her older brother, Steve, waved at her impatiently.

Not bothering to waste the energy to answer, she dug the three tined fork into the windrow and added the long stalks to the stook she'd already half finished. If the weather held and the hay dried well, tomorrow one of her brothers would drive the big hay wagon to collect the stooks.

Methodically, the hay crew worked its way along the wavy lines of the windrows. The rhythmic clacking of the mower reached her from two fields away where Father walked behind Benny and Bessie, the big patient workhorses who pulled the mower. It was a blessing that field wouldn't require her attention until after it was raked in a day or two.

"Land sakes, haying does seem to take forever," Annie muttered, stabbing the pale green hump of partially dried grasses.

"Water, Miss Baldwin?"

"Oh my Lord!" Annie dropped the hayfork and put a hand to her chest. "George, you scared the life out of me." She bent to pick up the discarded tool and to avoid looking at the young man smiling at her.

"Would you like some water?" He held a wooden bucket with a ladle in it. "It's some hot today." George's English accent was different to her ear than Father and Mother's Irish inflections.

"Yes, I do believe I could do with some water, George. Thank you." Annie dipped the metal ladle into the warm water and drank, allowing some of the fluid to overflow and run down her neck into her bodice. She glanced out from under the brim of her bonnet and met his grey-eyed gaze. Offering him a faint smile she replaced the ladle in the bucket.

George touched his cap with a finger and then trudged down the row where Annie's older sisters were also tying bundles to build into stooks. She let her gaze linger on the boy. Father borrowed him from the Millers who farmed closer to Eganville. Her ears still blistered from Mother's lecture last evening. Annie shook her head and returned to the task-at-hand, letting her thoughts wander as her body methodically went through the motions. She was at a loss to understand why Mother was so upset over Annie exchanging a few words with the English boy at the end of work yesterday. Heavens they'd known each other for years, attended the same one room school before they grew too old. Why should Mother suddenly get such a bee in her bonnet over an innocent conversation?

Why should it matter if he was basically nothing more than an indentured servant? He was nice enough and worked hard, harder than most of her brothers, and certainly George did more work than her sisters. Annie reached the end of her row and stepped across to work her way along the next windrow back the way she had come. In the distance the waters of the Bonnechere River glittered in the afternoon sun, trees lining its borders stood motionless in the muggy June afternoon.

"I'd give my eye teeth to go jump in the river right about now," she muttered. Not much chance of that happening. Annie paused to stretch her back, straightening up she glanced across the field to gauge how close they were to finishing this field. If they kept at it, they'd be done by dusk, she calculated. With any luck, her sister Rotha would have milked the cows and fed the pigs and chickens. She always managed to knock off before the rest of them and head back to the house on some frail excuse or another. If those chores weren't done, it would fall to Annie as the youngest, to make sure they got done. She sighed, there was no telling when the woman would decide to pull her 'lady of the manner' act and decide such chores were beneath her.

The red ball of sun in the hazy sky was just brushing the tips of the trees lining the river when Father stopped the mower by the gate. Annie stood the last bundle into her stook and trudged toward him. The two-acre field was dotted with upright cones of hay placed in wavering lines across the shorn grasses. She caught up to Steve and Evan, falling into step with her brothers. George joined them and they came to a halt where Father sat on the metal seat of the mower. Benny and Bessie stood hip-shot, eyes half-closed, tails swishing at the ever-present flies. It was odd how her father preferred to walk with the horses rather than ride, finding it easier on the body when the iron wheels hit gopher and rabbit holes perhaps.

"Time to call it a day," Father declared. He clucked to the team and slapped the lines lightly on their rumps. With a jingle of harness and machinery the mower bumped down the grassy lane.

Steve and Evan outpaced Annie with their long limbed hill walker's gait. Too tired to attempt to keep up, she let them draw ahead of her. She glanced up at George as he matched his stride to hers. He swung the empty water bucket in his hand. The uneven ground and tired muscles conspired to throw her off balance and she took a misstep, lurching a bit and bumping against him. Heat and electricity flared through Annie, she drew back as if she'd bumped into the pot belly of the wood stove. George caught her elbow and steadied her, his face colouring more than the heat and sunburn could account for.

"I'm so sorry," she managed to say.

He shook his head and released her arm, avoiding her eyes. "Think nothing of it."

When they reached the bank barn, Father handed George the lines with instructions to unhitch the team and make them comfortable for the night. A pang of sympathy lanced through Annie at the realization he would still have the mower to clean and oil before he would see any supper. Her eyes followed his progress to the barn, one hand resting on Bessie's broad shoulder as he paced beside the big horses. Even though his shoulders hunched with exhaustion and his gait uneven, somehow he seemed happy.

"Annabelle!" Father growled. "Quit lallygagging about and go help with supper."

She spun around and hurried to the house to change and wash. Please don't let Father mention to Mother I was looking at George. I don't think I can stomach another lecture right now. My belly is touching my backbone I'm so hungry. Annie hurried to the room she shared with two of her sisters and shucked her work clothes, taking them outside to shake the chaff and seed heads out of the long skirts and underskirts once she'd dressed appropriately for supper. Folding them neatly she left them on the clothes press by the wall. Tomorrow was another day.

* * *

Supper was a quiet affair, with everyone too tired to do more than eat. Mother sat primly at the opposite end of the table from Father looking like she was presiding over high tea. She appeared fresh as a daisy in spite of the fact she'd been adding rennet to the current batch of cheese for most of the afternoon. Annie rose when the men wandered off to take their leisure. In no time flat she had the table cleared. Piling them in the dry sink, she took the bucket from under the wooden frame and went toward the back door heading for the well in the yard.

"Annabelle!"

She stopped short at Mother's summons and turned. A tin bucket covered with a square of cloth was thrust into her hands.

"Since you've got to go out anyway, take this out to the workers bunked in the barn. Mind you don't dawdle and don't be fraternizing with that orphan boy. You're better than that, child. Heavens, the boy's an orphan and came over as a Doctor Barnardo boy, who knows what he picked up on the streets of Liverpool. Or on the ship." Mother shuddered genteelly and gave her daughter a push. "Get along with you, girl. Mind you stay away from the younger brother as well. You hear me?"

"Yes, Mother." Annie hooked the water bucket over her arm and held the pail with the workers' bait against her side. Might as well deliver the food first, she reasoned. The three hired men must be hungry. Thank the good Lord the others who lived nearer went home at night.

10

Dusk deepened to a darker twilight, a warm spread of buttery yellow spilled out the part-open door of the barn.

"Hello!" Annie hesitated, not wanting to walk in on something she shouldn't be seeing. "I've brought supper."

Amos' grizzled face peered around the door before he swung it open. "C'min, c'min, lass." The stocky Irishman grinned at her and waved her into the dim interior. "There's a crate over to the wall where you can put that there bucket."

She moved carefully over the straw and hay strewn floor. The rich summer scent of fresh cut hay hung in the close air. It was slightly cooler now the sun was down, but the heat lingered in the sultry night. Annie set the tin pail on the crate and turned to go.

Her breath caught in her throat when her gaze fell on the long lean muscles of George's back as he sluiced water over his head. The moisture gleamed in the lamplight, the waistband of his trousers black where the water soaked them. He raised his head, eyes wide like a startled deer. Snatching a ragged towel from a nail in the beam beside him, he held it to his chest like a shield.

"I'm sorry, Miss Baldwin. I had no idea you were here. Please don't mind me." The Adam's apple bobbled in his throat.

"Of course," she managed to stutter, tearing her gaze from his wiry frame. His ribs were visible; it was painfully obvious he could use more meat on his bones. Why Father feeds his dogs better. A wave of shame washed over her, although she had no say in how anyone was fed. "I brought supper." She waved an awkward hand toward the cloth covered pail. "I must…I must go…" Without lingering further, she hurried into the night.

The pale light of the half-moon allowed her to pick her way to the well without too much trouble. She drew the oak bucket up by the windlass and dumped the contents into her own bucket. Letting the empty bucket slip from her fingers she waited to hear it hit the water below with a hollow thump. Her achy muscles complained when she hefted the full bucket and lugged it into the kitchen.

"What took you so long, Annie?" Her older sister Hetty demanded, hands firmly planted on her hips. "You weren't out there sparking with that orphan English boy were you?"

"No, of course not!" She turned her back and heaved the water bucket onto the flat side of the dry sink.

"There's no future in it. He doesn't have a row to hoe except what belongs to someone else. You'll never get a man to ask for your hand if you ruin your reputation by taking up with the likes of him," Hetty declared.

"I just took the food out like I was told," Annie muttered ladling water into the sink. She added soap flakes when it was full enough and started in on the supper dishes, fully expecting her sister to pick up a dishtowel to dry them, it being her turn to do so.

Instead, Hetty sailed out of the kitchen. "Father has things he needs me to attend to," she called over her shoulder.

Her actions were nothing new, but the ease with which her sister escaped chores still scalded Annie. No sense appealing to Mother, Father's word was law. No need asking where Rotha was either. She sighed.

Chapter Two

The sun was still high in the western sky when Steve forked the last of the hay into the open doors of the loft. A fine sprinkling of hayseeds and dust danced in the golden slanted rays of the afternoon light. Annie pushed the bonnet back on her head and wiped the back of her hand across her forehead. Bits of chaff clung to her damp lashes and cheeks and itched terribly inside the confines of her bodice. Shaking the dust from her long skirts, Annie turned toward the house intending to slip behind the hen house and into the green shady bush of the shed hill. There was time before supper if she hurried and the Bonnechere River only required a short hike along a trail she knew.

Just a few minutes in the shallow pool under the willows by the bank would take care of the dust coating her everywhere and the infernal itching of hay chaff that seemed to have found its way into impossible nooks and crannies. Hay fork in hand, she got as far as the barn doors.

"Annabelle! Where do you think you're going?" Hetty called. Her sister strode across the rough pasture between barn and main house, not a hair out of place.

It was unchristian to think ill of a family member so Annie repressed the surge of anger and the names she wouldn't ever dare say out loud. Hetty was the apple of Father's eye and could do no wrong. Even if she did do something she shouldn't, somehow it was Annie who bore the brunt of Father's anger. Mother never spoke up in her defence, even though she knew the truth. Ella Baldwin would never say a word to contradict her husband.

"I'm just putting the fork up," Annie replied schooling her features into a pleasant mask. Drat, drat, drat! I swear she does it on purpose, just to vex me.

"Well, do it then. I need to speak with Father." Hetty swept on like a ship in full sail toward the now empty hay wagon.

Annie returned the hayfork to the barn and hesitated in the shadow of the door, her heart twisting a bit in her chest. George had his head tipped toward Hetty who was plainly flirting with him. Annie shook her head and stepped into the sunlight. If he only knew what Hetty really thought about him or said about him in private. To her surprise, George frowned and shook his head before he took a step back from her sister and touched a finger to his cap before moving to tend to the horses.

She moved out of the way as the wagon rattled toward her, George on the far side of the horses as they passed. Annie entertained the thought of helping unharness the team, she did so love the horses and Benny was her favourite.

Now that the possibility of a swim was out of the question, spending a few minutes with the horses would be a kind of reward. She might have known, like most of her wishes, it would come to naught.

"Annabelle!" Father waved an imperious hand at her.

"Coming, Father." Gritting her teeth and forcing a semblance of a smile, she made her way back to the cluster of men, and Hetty. The woman in question was looking particularly smug, which usually boded ill for Annie. "Yes, Father?" She halted a few feet from him, tipping her head so the brim of her hat partially blocked the sunlight streaming over the tall man's shoulders.

"Don't be running off, girl. I need you to take the buggy to town and pick up the mail. I'm expecting an important letter."

"But, Father—" She started to protest it was Rotha's turn to get the mail.

"None of your impertinence, girl. Do as you're told. I'll hear no more about it."

"Yes, Father," she replied and turned on her heel, seething inside but not daring to let it show.

"Annabelle!"

She stopped and turned back, clenched fists hidden in the dusty folds of her skirts. "Yes, Father?"

"Be sure to take George Richardson with you and drop him at the Millers on your way past. No reason to go down the lane, just drop the boy at the foot. I'll see that Miller gets his wages by week end. Oh, and take his brother too, drop him at Munroe's." He turned his back in dismissal.

"Yes, Father," she repeated and turned back toward the barn. It didn't seem fair that poor George and Peter did all the hard labour, but Annie'd bet her best dress the boys would never see a penny of the wages. Still the Millers weren't the worst, at least they kept George sort of fed and clothed by the look of him. The younger brother's clothes were clean but patched and his bony wrists showed below the sleeves of the too small shirt. If anything, Peter seemed thinner than his brother. Annie sighed, the Munroes could barely keep themselves, little wonder they were hiring out the young orphan boy they'd taken in. At least the brothers ended up fairly close to each other, they were luckier than most.

She entered the shadowy barn and stopped to let her eyes adjust to the dim light. Long beams of sunlight shot through the gaps in the wall. Her brothers would have to patch things before the snow flew, she mused.

"Mister Richardson? Oh, there you are."

The English boy stepped out from behind Bessie, a dandy brush in hand. "Hallo, Miss Baldwin. What is it I can help you with?"

"Father has asked me to drive into Eganville to fetch the mail. He wants me to drop you at the Millers, and your brother at Monroe's on the way." She ducked her head when his expression brightened. "Would you be so kind as to catch Molly from the pasture and hitch her to the buggy? Oh, where is your brother, by the way?"

"Peter's waiting for me by the end of the lane. He forgot his bait pail where we stopped for lunch. If he doesn't take it back there'll be no lunch for him tomorrow." George hesitated, glancing from the brush in his hand to the horse beside him. Shaking his head, he put the brush on the edge of a stall, gathered a head collar and lead shank from the front of another and disappeared out a man door on the side of the building.

Annie picked up the brush and finished grooming the stocky mare. Benny was already clean and had his head buried in a mound of hay. "C'mon, boy." She pulled his head up and led the two horses out to the west pasture where she slipped their head collars off and turned them loose. Slinging the leather halters over her shoulder Annie returned to the barn and hung the halters where they belonged. The work harness was already in its place, but one of her brothers would have to clean it after supper. She'd bet her bottom dollar on that, if she had one.

"Come along then, miss." George led Molly into the barn and gave her a quick brush, before backing her between the shafts of the buggy.

"I must run up to the house and see if Mother needs anything at Arlo's," Annie called before hurrying toward the house. If she went to town without checking to see if anything was needed for the household she'd never hear the end of it.

Leaving the house with the list clutched in hand, Annie lifted her skirts and ran across the yard. Ivan followed at her heels, Mother declaring her daughter was not about to go driving off unchaperoned with two field hands. George was just leading Molly into the barn yard when she arrived, slightly out of breath. "Just in time," she greeted him. Shoving the list into her pocket she hitched her skirts and climbed into the buggy before George could come around to help her. He joined her on the narrow seat, careful not to let his thigh touch her skirts. Ivan hopped in the back, hanging his legs off the tailgate.

"I could ride in the back if you wish, Miss Baldwin," George offered, avoiding meeting her eye.

"Don't be silly, Mister Richardson. You're fine where you are."

"Your father...I don't want to appear over familiar with a daughter of the house, like," he insisted.

Annie glanced toward the house, but Father must have already gone to wash up. "If it makes you more comfortable then by all means ride in the back. It seems so ridiculous for you not to just stay where you are."

"It's a class thing, miss. Surely you see that? The Millers, and your father, are kind to me, but I know me place and take care to stay in it."

Annie clucked to the mare and set off down the lane to the Eganville road. In the distance the Bonnechere River glistened between its green banks. She sighed in regret, wishing she'd managed to slip away for a swim earlier. Class, knowing your place. It all seems so horribly unfair. A person's birth surely shouldn't dictate and limit their opportunities to better themselves.

"Do you miss Liverpool over there in England?" She glanced at the silent boy beside her. His work roughened hands were clasped in his lap.

"In some ways. Not in others," he replied.

Annie glanced at him with a frown. He didn't seem inclined to enlarge on his brief reply. "Ho, Molly." She pulled the mare to a halt beside the stocky youth leaning on the gatepost. "You can ride in the back, Peter Richardson. Father has asked me to give you a ride as far as the end of the Monroe's lane."

Peter touched a finger to the brim of his sweat-stained cap. Swinging the bait pail by its strap he tossed it into the wagon bed and hitched himself up onto the rough boards of the buggy bed. "Thankee, miss. It's a sigh better'n walkin'." He settled beside Ivan and the two put their heads together, whispering and giggling over something.

"Will you boys be coming to the Dominion Day celebrations?" Annie was careful not to look directly at the silent youth beside her. From the corner of her eye she caught the flush of red that darkened his already sunburned face.

"Miz Munroe says we're all goin'," Peter Richardson answered her from his perch on the tailgate. "You're comin', aren't you Georgie?"

"Don't know. And don't call me Georgie." George shifted on the hard bench, his fingers clenched on the rough fabric of his trousers.

"Surely, the Millers will allow you to attend?" Annie dared to look directly at him. "I heard Mother telling Father she'd spoken to Mrs. Miller and they were planning to attend."

"Don't rightly know, miss," George mumbled.

"You still in hot water over that Amelia girl?" Peter chirped from behind.

"Go on with you," George snarled. "That ain't none of your business, Pete. Leave it alone."

Annie regarded him thoughtfully. "The oldest Miller girl giving you trouble?"

He shrugged and turned to glare at his younger brother. He was saved from further inquiries by their arrival at the foot of the Munroe's lane. Annie pulled the buggy to halt and waited for her passenger to jump off the tailgate.

"Did Father say if he needed you tomorrow?" She looked down on the curly head of the boy who loitered by the side of the buggy.

Peter nodded. "Mister Baldwin wants the corn crib cleared out, and the chicken house needs cleaning. Said he'd arrange it with old man Munroe." He glanced toward the sun disappearing quickly behind the treetops. "Gotta get a move on, still got me chores to do to home. See ya in the mornin', George?" Peter scuffed a bare foot in the sandy dust of the road.

"Reckon so. 'Less the Millers have other plans for me. You go on ahead if I don't show in the mornin'. Don't wait on me."

"Sure. Night then, George. Miss." Peter pulled on the bill of his cap and nodded at Annie.

"Good night, Peter. Do be careful in the morning, Father mentioned he'd seen wolf tracks by the sheep fold yesterday."

"Ain't no wolf gonna bother me, miss." Peter laughed and headed up the sandy lane with a careless wave.

"Giddup, Molly." Annie slapped the lines lightly on the mare's rump. With a sigh the horse leaned into the harness and the buggy lurched forward.

"Do you really think the Millers won't let you come to the Dominion Day do?"

The boy at her side shrugged again and avoided her gaze.

"What did Amelia say that got you in heck with Mister Miller? I promise I won't breathe a word of it to anyone. I'm always getting in trouble for things that aren't my fault, but Father won't hear a word against Hetty, and if she says I did or didn't do something…Well, Father uses his belt first and doesn't want to hear any excuses…" She was getting breathless from blethering on, but somehow couldn't seem to stop the torrent of words vomiting out of her mouth.

"Do you always talk so much? And so fast?" George shifted on the seat to actually look at her.

Heat flashed up her neck and her ears burned. "I…no…not usually…I mean…nobody ever listens to me… I'm sorry." She broke off and blinked to keep the embarrassed tears from escaping her lashes.

"No, it's me that's sorry. That was unforgivably rude of me. Please don't tell your Father or I'll not get any work from him and old man Miller will take it out of my hide." His grey eyes held her captive for a moment before he dropped his gaze.

"Oh no! I won't say anything to Father. I promise." She paused and then pressed on. "Does Mister Miller really beat you?"

George nodded wordlessly.

"How awful! I mean Father takes a belt to me when I anger him, but he's my father and it's his right to mete out discipline. But…"

"But the Millers own me, lock, stock and barrel. Until I'm of age and there's nothing I can do about it." His face twisted bitterly.

"How did you end up at Doctor Barnardo's? Did you have no family in Liverpool who would take you in?" Annie swatted at the mosquitoes that swarmed as they passed into the part of the low part of the road over shadowed with tall trees.

"There were family all right, just none who wanted us. Peter and me, I mean."

"Was it a small family then?" Annie's interest was piqued, his English accent seemed exotic and somehow exciting and she wanted to keep him talking.

"My da was the youngest of thirteen. Not one of them took any interest in us a'tall after he popped his cogs. Just Uncle James, he's the one what got us into the Liverpool Sheltering Home and Barnardo's. Done the best by us he could, I guess." George glanced at her as if defying her to pity him.

"What was it like? At the home, I mean." Annie kept her eyes on the mare's rump moving rhythmically before her.

"It were all right, I guess. Fed us and put clothes on our backs. Made us go to school some." He chewed on the side of his thumb nail.

"Were they mean to you?"

"Not on purpose like, no. There were so many of us no one paid any mind to us unless we was bad or turned up missing."

"Missing?"

"The home is in London's east end, lots of street kids trying to stay alive by selling matches and flowers, sweeping the street for the toffs to cross. If ye was lucky ye could get on with a gang who had a territory to collect dog shit…beggin' yer pardon fer m'language, miss."

24

"Dog poop? Why would you collect that?" Annie shifted to look directly at him. "You pulling my leg?"

"On my word, I'm not. The tanners use it to cure the hides. Pures they call it."

"Ewww." Annie wrinkled her nose. "It's bad enough turning the cow patties and horse manure into the garden in the spring and fall, and using it to help chink logs, but dog...Ewww."

"It's not so bad when you know it'll get you a few pennies and food in yer belly." George shrugged.

"How did—Whoa, mare! Ho!" Annie sawed on the lines as the little mare shied violently to the right and attempted to bolt.

"Let her go! Let her go! Look!" George pointed to the bushes at the side of the road. His work-roughened hands closed over hers and wrested the lines from her.

Annie gripped the side of the buggy seat, her heart in her throat. The black bear surged out of the thick raspberry brambles lining this part of the road, her two cubs close behind her. "Dear Lord." She clung to the seat while George sent the buggy careening down the dirt road. She glanced behind after a moment once she'd had a chance to gather her thoughts and slow her racing heart. "She's not chasing us, I think it's safe now." She laid a hand on his forearm, the muscles like steel bands beneath her fingers.

George slowed the still flighty mare to a prancing walk. "There, my pet. 'Tis, all right now. Easy now, pet." He soothed the mare and Molly settled to a walk shaking her head hard enough to set the bridle chiming.

Annie took the lines back and pulled the mare to a halt at the foot of the Miller's lane. "Here you are." She glanced the way they had come with a nervous twitch. *What if the she bear is still there when I drive home?*

"You worried about that old bear?" George made no move to get off the seat.

She nodded, ashamed of herself for being such a coward. *Father would tell her to keep a stiff upper lip and get on with it. Fear and bear be-damned.*

"You want I should ride into Eganville with you and back this far? There's enough daylight left so the Millers won't be expectin' me home just yet. They'll be expecting me to walk from your place."

"Would you?" Relief made her light-headed and a bit ashamed of her fear. "Are you sure you won't catch heck because of it? I don't want to get you in trouble, or me either, if Mister Miller tells Father I made you late getting back."

"What the mind doesn't know, the heart can't grieve over." He grinned at her, grey eyes warming to silver in the dim light under the trees.

"I think I would like that very much." Annie turned to fix her brother with a stern stare. "Mind you don't say anything to Father about this, you hear? It's just to make sure we don't run into any trouble with that momma bear on the way home."

Ivan met her gaze solemnly. "Cross my heart." He suited action to words. "Promise."

"All right, then. Git up, Molly." She shook the lines at the patient mare who broke into a sprightly trot which made Ivan squeal with laughter and clutch the side of the buggy box.

The road took a turn just before the town came into sight. George shifted uneasily and cleared his throat. Annie glanced at him and pulled the mare to halt. "Is something wrong?"

"It might be best if I wait for you here. Word travels…" He let his words trail off.

"I suppose you are probably right about that. Those gossip Gerties would love to have something to fill Hetty or Mother's ears with about me. Are you sure you'll be all right waiting here?" She glanced at the thick brush bordering the road. "The flies will eat you alive, I'm afraid."

George jumped down into the dust and grinned up at her. "I'll be just fine, miss. You just stop somewheres nearby on your way back. I'll be waiting."

"If you're quite sure…"

"Time's a'wasting. You best get a move on." George slapped the mare lightly on the rump and disappeared into the raspberry brambles and choke cherry bushes.

Leaving Ivan to watch the buggy, Annie made short work of collecting the mail. There was a big box of something heavy for Father from Ireland along with a batch of papers and letters. She stashed them under the seat of the buggy before going to Arlo's to purchase the items on Mother's list. She returned shortly after with a bag of flour balanced on one shoulder and the rest of the items weighing down the basket in her other hand.

"There, all done." She heaved the basket into the back of the buggy and flipped the flour down beside it. A fine dusting of white powder puffed out of the canvas bag. "Mind you don't get that all over you, Ivan," she cautioned her brother. "Come ride up here with me." She patted the wooden seat beside her.

"Can I drive?" Ivan clambered over the back of the bench and plopped down at her side.

"No. Not in town, for sure." Annie shook her head. "You know Father says you're still too young to drive the buggy."

Ivan stuck his lower lip out in belligerence before glancing at her sideways. Annie's stomach clenched at the sly expression on her brother's young face. It was like looking at smaller male version of Hetty at her worst. "Of course I understand, you wouldn't want to cross Father, would you?" He studiously picked at some lint on his trouser leg. "I'm sure Father will understand why the English boy rode into town with you. Don't you think?" Ivan turned innocent guileless eyes on her.

She hesitated for a moment, weighing her options. By rights, she should tell the little fiend to go chase himself. However, he was a Baldwin

28

through and through with the tenacious stubbornness and willfulness to stop at nothing to get what he wanted. Damn. He'll run right to Father before I can get the buggy unhitched.

"Well?"

"Fine." Annie heaved a sigh. "Once we get clear of town you can drive for a bit. Mind you don't breathe a word of this to anyone or we'll both get our arses tanned."

"I thought you'd see it my way." Ivan regarded her with a smug smile.

"Don't push your luck," she warned him. "Git up with you, Molly."

The buggy rolled down the road following the river. As soon as they cleared the outskirts Ivan began bouncing on the seat. "Now? Now? Can I now?"

"Hush, Ivan. You can take the lines after we find George."

"Oh all right." The boy crossed his arms over his chest and huffed with impatience.

Scanning the brush crowding the edges of the road, Annie stopped at the point where she thought they'd left the English boy. "Hush, Ivan," she commanded before he had a chance to whine again. "George? It's us, come out!"

The bushes crackled and trembled behind her. The mare threw up her head and bunched her hindquarters. Annie swallowed against the tightness in her throat. What if it's another bear? Or... Fingers tight on the lines, she held the mare in check, ready to urge her forward if the shaker in the bushes wasn't who she hoped it was.

George pushed free of the brambles and jogged to the buggy. "I thought you'd missed me." His voice was a little breathless.

"It took longer than I anticipated at Arlo's. Climb up, I want to be home before full dark. Shove over, Ivan."

George put a foot on the wheel hub and levered himself onto the buggy. He started to sling a leg over the sideboard of the wagon bed.

"Sit up here with us," Annie invited. "Stop that!" She hissed at her brother who stuck his sharp bony elbow in her ribs. Sometimes the old-fashioned stiff corset Mother insisted she wear had its advantages. Not often though, she sighed again.

"Not 'til you let me drive," Ivan insisted.

"Fine, here." She handed him the lines. "Be careful now, and keep your mind on what you're doing."

"I know what I'm doing," he declared. "Haven't I driven the work team when we're picking up stooks?" Ivan clucked to the mare, who moved forward at a slow pace, but not before turning her head to glance at Annie as if to question her sanity.

George squeezed in between her and the far edge of the narrow seat. He unconsciously scratched at the back of his neck.

"Were the bugs bad in the bush?" Annie waved a hand to chase away a swarm of

30

mosquitoes that rose from the wet land the road dipped down into.

"Feel like a pin cushion, the beggars got a good meal out of me." He offered a rueful grin.

Molly plodded along, ignoring Ivan slapping the lines on her rump. Annie twisted her hands in the folds of her skirts, at a loss for words. The uneasy silence continued, wearing on her nerves until she couldn't stand it any longer. "Do try and come to the Dominion Day celebrations," she blurted out the first thing that came to mind, immediately mentally kicking herself for being over eager. Heavens above, what will he think of me? Mother would claim I'm leading him on by showing such interest. She bit her lower lip, hating the heat that rose in her face.

"Aye, well. I'll do my best. Pete is almost positive the Munroes are planning on bringing him along." George paused and sighed, a calloused hand rubbing at the thin stubble on his cheeks.

"I do hope you will be able to attend...I mean it would be nice for you and your brother to be able to spend some time together and get a break from working all the time. Ivan, pull up here, please." Annie put a hand over her brother's and Molly ambled to a halt at the foot of the Miller's lane.

George jumped down and looked up at her, the last vestiges of the late afternoon sun highlighting his ruddy complexion. "I'll do my best, miss." He touched a finger to the grimy bill of his cap and hurried away before Annie could say anything more.

"Here, give me the lines." Annie wrested the reins away from her brother's grip. "It's not far now, no point in taking the chance of anyone seeing you driving. I can get in enough trouble without any help from you. Remember, you promised to keep your mouth shut about Miller's help riding all the way into Eganville with us."

"Sure." Ivan nodded, his expression non-committal.

I'll strangle him with my bare hands if he makes a peep. "Git along, Molly."

Chapter Three

July 1st 1916 Dominion Day celebrations were a bit more subdued than previous years. The war to end all wars as H.G. Wells declared on August 14, 1914 was well into its second year of conflict. Luxury items were starting to become scarce. But in the small town of Eganville, Ontario on the Bonnechere River things weren't as impacted as they were in larger centres.

The harvest promised to be a bumper crop this year, so optimism was high. Annie shoved her hat pin deeper into the nest of her hair, hoping to keep the new straw hat from coming adrift. She was crammed in the bed of the buckboard with her siblings. Except for Hetty, of course. Riding with a gaggle of siblings was beneath Hetty Baldwin newly betrothed to Clarence Hiram. Dust rose from the well-travelled road, everyone from the surrounding countryside seemed to be headed into town. She leaned over the side of the wagon and peered ahead. Thank goodness, they were almost there. Once Father found a strategic place to park the buckboard, Annie planned to slip away into the crowd and avoid being saddled with her younger sibling. Rotha was two years older than her and could take her turn looking after the little heathen.

On another note, Annie wanted to be out of earshot when Father clambered up onto the back of the wagon and began his hell fire and brimstone preaching. While she admired his convictions and his passion, it was more than a little embarrassing when he got so enraptured that spittle flew from his mouth. The wagon jolted to a halt and she hurried to disembark, being careful not to snag her full skirts on the heel of her new boots. She admired them for a moment before shaking her skirts down to cover all but the toe. It wouldn't do for Mother to seize the opportunity to lecture her about vanity or showing her ankles.

Giving her skirts one last shake to remove the dust, Annie twisted the strings of the small crocheted purse securely around her wrist. Hetty's high clear voice preceded her appearance prompting Annie to slip between two groups of gossiping older women and make good her escape from family responsibility. She grinned while putting more space between herself and the wagon. Surely Hetty's voice could cut glass, given the chance. Stifling a giggle she wriggled past the crowded doorway into Arlo's General Store. With her small hoard of pennies she purchased some licorice whips and peppermint sticks. Not wishing to linger and be discovered by her siblings who were sure to be headed in this direction, Annie left the establishment as unobtrusively as possible. She paused on the boardwalk outside, deciding the best place to observe the official celebrations without peering around tall people and taller hats.

"Annie…Miss Baldwin, how nice to see you."

The voice at her elbow set her heart racing. "My Lord, you near scared the life out of me," she exclaimed. Pressing a hand to her chest, she smiled at young man. "It's a pleasure to see you as well, Peter Richardson."

"I was looking for my brother. You haven't seen George, have you?"

Annie shook her head. "I just got here myself. Shall we see if we can find him in this crowd?"

"If that's what you would like," Peter sounded a bit surprised but gallantly offered her his arm.

"I think I would like that very much." Annie tucked her hand into the crook of his elbow.

The humid July air curled the tendrils of hair escaping from her hat where they stuck against her cheek. The new dress was becoming, but Lord it was hot. Even the backs of her knees were sweating under her lisle stockings. Annie took a deep breath, inhaling the mingled scents of food, hot humans, some of which didn't seem to have bathed, dust and the acrid odour of horse manure. With her free hand she wiped her face with the silly scrap of lace Mother deemed was the only handkerchief a lady should be seen in possession of. She stuffed it back up her sleeve and allowed Peter to break a path for them through the throng.

"George!" Peter shouted before turning to glance at her. "There he is." He pointed where his brother stood perched atop a barrel to get a better view of the goings on. "George!"

"Petey, I thought I'd never find you in this crowd. And Miss Baldwin, too! What a nice surprise." George jumped down from his barrel. His spot being taken immediately by another youth. "We'd best get out of the way," he remarked at the sound of the marching band approaching.

Annie gathered her long skirts and stepped up onto the porch of the harness maker they were standing in front of. Conversation was quite impossible for a few moments, she was very aware of George as the crowd strained for a better look and jostled her against him. His hand caught her elbow to steady her, for a second she leaned into his solid strength. The fingers on her arm tightened, Annie glanced up to find his grey eyes looking down at her, a strange and oddly exciting expression on his face. Something fluttered in her belly, startled at the unfamiliar and vaguely frightening sensation, she pulled away and dropped her gaze.

"Look the speeches are about to start." Peter seemed oblivious to whatever it was that was happening between his brother and Annie. A fact she was eternally grateful for. Somehow, she wanted to keep it a secret, at least until she figured out exactly what she was feeling and what she was to do about it.

Her feet were starting to hurt in the new button up boots. Annie would much preferred to wear her old comfortable ones, but Mother, supported by Hetty, declared it would never do for a Baldwin to appear at Dominion Day in anything less than perfect attire. Why didn't Rotha ever speak up, she wondered. Or Alice? Both her sisters were older than her, but younger than Hetty. There were enough years between them that Rotha and Alice never bothered much with their younger sister. Maybe it was because as long as Mother and Hetty were picking on Annie, they weren't paying any attention to Rotha and Alice.

"Excuse me?" She turned to Peter who tugged on her sleeve.

"I asked if you'd like to find some place cooler."

"Oh?" She peeked out of the corner of her eye at George, standing silent by her other side.

"Unless you'd rather listen to the speeches?" Peter looked uncertain. "I was thinkin' it would be cooler down by the river..."

Annie glanced around, she spotted her tall brothers towering over the crowd. Mother and the girls wouldn't be far from them. Ivan could be anywhere, the boy was always scampering off on his own, but he didn't appear to be in her vicinity at the moment. Still, what would Mother say if word got back to her that her youngest daughter had gone off with two basically indentured servants? Father would take the belt to her, for sure. Annie settled her hat more firmly over her eyes to block the blistering heat of the sun and plucked at the high neck of her dress. The thought of stripping off the pinching shoes and itching stockings and plunging her aching feet into the cool water was more than tempting. Common sense warred with her rebellious side. Usually, aided by the fear of retribution, common sense won out. But today…the heat was so oppressive the air had weight to it.

"What do you say, Annie?" Peter broke into her contemplations. "Owww! What'd you do that for?" He scowled at his brother.

"Mind your tongue, lad. It's Miss Baldwin and well you know it." George tweaked the younger boy's ear.

"Gerrof!" Peter swatted at him. "Sorry, miss," he mumbled.

"Oh for heaven's sake! I've known you boys for years all this formality is silly. Call me Annie…both of you."

George shook his head, a crease of worry wrinkling his forehead. "Can't, miss. Not where anyone can hear at least. Old man Miller be sure to remind me of my place in society. And Munroe would do worse by Petey."

Annie frowned, George made the word society sound like a cuss word. "Well, I'm not society." She matched his tone and stamped her foot, immediately regretting it as the boot pinched her toes. "I insist you call me by my Christian name, at least when we're not around anyone who'll get us into trouble over it."

"C'mon, Georgie. What can it hurt?" Peter wheedled. "I ain't afraid of Mister Munroe."

"You should be. He essentially owns you until you're eighteen, remember? That's what they both say, so it must be true," George reminded his brother.

"That's only until next April. I can stand it that long. What about you, you're of age now, why don't you just up and leave?" Peter demanded.

"You know why," George mumbled and picked at his thumb.

Peter snorted and shook his head. "I can take care of myself. Don't need you to hang around just for me."

Annie looked from one brother to the other. There was more going on behind the words but darned if she could figure out what it was. At any rate the conversation was somewhat unsettling, though she couldn't put her finger on exactly what it was that making her feel that way. The speeches droned on in the background and her head was starting to ache from the heat. "I think going to the river sounds like a good idea." She broke into the boys' conversation.

"Really?" Peter spun toward her. "You mean it? C'mon. Let's go."

"I can't think of anything I'd like more," Annie replied firmly shoving thoughts of parental upset from her mind. She wriggled her way toward the back of the crowd and once the throng of bodies lessened she caught up with Peter who had bolted the moment he heard her approval of his plan. Glancing over her shoulder, she smiled encouragement at George whose expression told her he was of two minds about the wisdom of their actions.

Once they were free of the crowd the heat was marginally less although the faint breeze did little more than shift the humid air. Annie followed Peter along the beaten path through the bushes and trees lining the river bank. They came to a clearing where the path stuck out into the river. Peter was already sitting on the grassy hummocks shedding his shoes and stockings. He rolled the legs of his best pants up past his knees. Annie tried not to stare at the skinny shanks his actions revealed. She plunked down with a sigh of relief and struggled with the stiff button hooks of her new boots. George's presence behind her set her heart jumping. Pulling the first boot off, she wriggled feeling back into her toes. Instruments of torture, that's what the cursed things were, she decided. Being careful not to expose too much ankle she rolled the stocking down and shoved it into the boot by her side before tackling the other foot.

Peter was already wading in the shallows at the river edge being careful not to venture into deeper water where the current was strong. Both feet now free, Annie dug her feet into the sandy soil of the bank, letting the coolness soothe the ache caused by the new boots. Her face heated uncomfortably when she caught George staring at her ankles below the hem of her skirts.

She tossed her head and pulled the straw hat free of her straggling hair, setting it beside her on the grass. I don't care, it's too dratted hot to care about a friend seeing my ankles. Heavens above, some of the new styles actually leave the ankles bare on purpose. If only Mother wasn't so caught in the past. Although to be fair, it's probably Father more than her.

"Are you coming in?" Peter held his hand out to her.

"I believe I will." She grasped his work roughened hand and let him pull her upright. Letting go and using both hands she gathered the full skirts and underskirts in both hands, keeping the hem just below her knees. Carefully, she stepped into the shallows, where the water ran clear and rippled over the sand. Peter kept a hand under her elbow until she was steady on her feet. "Oh my, this feels wonderful." She closed her eyes and tipped her head back, long hair coming free of its knot and swishing down her back to brush her hips.

"Aren't you coming in, George?" She spoke without opening her eyes.

"I thought I should keep watch, warn you if someone happens by."

"Don't be silly. We aren't doing any harm, and anyways it's too darn hot to care."

"Mister Baldwin wouldn't see it that way, nor Mister Miller I imagine," he replied.

"A pox on them both," Annie said airily. "They'll be too busy listening to the speechifying, and Father will be itching to get up on the buckboard and preach fire and brimstone."

"Miss Baldwin!" George sounded indignant. "You shouldn't speak of your father like that."

"It's Annie, and it's true. He's never happier than when he's off on a rant about our sins and how we're all going to burn in hell. I figure if I'm gonna burn anyway, I might as well enjoy what I can before that happens."

"I don't imagine you speak like that where your father can hear you." His voice was stiff with disapproval.

"Of course not, but that doesn't mean I don't think it," she replied tartly. "Stay on the bank and roast then if that's what makes you happy." Annie opened her eyes and stepped out farther into the river, letting the water ripple around her ankles.

Peter stood knee deep in the river, sunlight turning his blonde hair to molten gold in the afternoon light. Sunlight the dappled the water with flickering shadows of the leaves that moved in the light breeze generated by the river current. Annie giggled as minnows nibbled at her toes darting shadows across the sunlit sandy bottom.

"You know…" Peter looked downriver and then over her head at his older brother behind her on the bank. "There's a row boat, just down there." He pointed. "We could borrow it and go to the sinkhole by the caverns. It's always cool in there…"

"What caverns? I don't think I've ever been there. How far is it?" Annie let the happiness of the afternoon carry her away.

"A ways. They're about five or six miles, I reckon. Not too far if we take the boat. C'mon, George. It'll be fun. The river runs over some rapids for a ways."

Annie turned tipped her head back to look at the boy on the bank. "Can we? I've never seen the sink hole. It might be the same one Steve and Evan talk about when they think Father isn't listening."

George looked over his shoulder before dropping unto his butt in the grass and peeling off his battered shoes and darned socks. Tying the laces together he slung them over his shoulder after stuffing his socks inside. "Let's go then." He jumped off the bank splashing Annie and Peter in the process.

Peter whooped with excitement and went to untie the painter and drag the row boat to where Annie waited. She tossed her boots into the bottom of the boat and gripped the gunwale with one hand. One side of her dress slipped into the water, but Annie was beyond caring. Hang it, I'll worry about it later. A squeak of surprise escaped her when strong arms lifted her and set her on the middle seat.

"Thanks, George," she managed to get out, although it sounded thin and breathless even to her.

He grinned at her and then turned his attention to helping Peter turn the bow of the boat downstream. Annie gripped the sides as the vessel dipped beneath her when George and Peter clambered aboard. Peter took one of the oars and poled the small wooden boat into the current which took hold of it and propelled it down river. The motion produced a welcome cooling breeze that lifted Annie's hair from her face and cooled her sun heated face. Too late she realized she'd left the straw hat in the shade of the river bank. Freckles, I'll get freckles. Hetty's always going on about freckles. What's so bad about a few freckles? She twisted on the narrow seat to find George's intense gaze fixed on her. Unable to resist, Annie gave him a brilliant smile and flicked water from her fingers at him.

Surprisingly, he returned her smile and dipped the oar he held into the water to splash her. Giggling, Annie wiped the moisture from her face and turned her face back in the direction they were headed. Peter stood in the bow striking a pose like a ragged bow sprite, if indeed bow sprites had been male.

"How will you know when we get there?" The freedom of coasting down the river on the current was so wonderful Annie would be content to just keep on going until they reached Renfrew. Even the rolling of the white water at the chutes didn't faze her. Laughing she gripped the gunwales and leaned forward.

"Don't worry, I know where it is. There's a certain cliff where the limestone is a different colour, and there's a huge waterfall."

"Waterfalls? We're not taking this," she indicated the little row boat with a wave of her hand, "down any waterfalls, are we?" Annie sat up straighter and tightened her grip on the gunwale.

"We're not goin' down any falls, Miss...I mean Annie. Not if I have anything to say about it," George assured her.

His words comforted her, she trusted in his solid strength and steadiness. Peter was closer to her age and more inclined to take chances than his older brother. For a moment her thoughts turned to the war. It seemed almost sinful to be enjoying the summer sun and the beauty of the river, when in the trenches of France and Belgium soldiers were dying and bombs were falling with no regard for life in any form. If Steve and Evan had their way they'd have enlisted already, only the fact that Father insisted they could do more for the war effort by staying on the farm and producing food kept them at home.

"There it is!" Peter pointed at an odd formation in the limestone beside the river.

As they drew nearer Annie leaned forward in amazement, the water flowed from the river into an opening in the bottom of the cliff and disappeared. "Where does it go?"

"Into the caves my friend Tom showed me," Peter said. He moved to join his brother at the oars, grunting with the effort of slowing the forward motion of the boat enough to angle it toward where he wanted to land. Annie saw the wisdom of keeping the boat near the edge of the river where the current was weak rather than out in the middle where the water rolled and moved at a much faster pace.

"George, shove over with your oar, would you? Hah! Got it!" Peter caught an overhanging branch of a maple tree and pulled the boat up against the bank, grounding it in the shallows.

His brother stepped out of the stern, muttering under his breath when he misjudged the depth of the water and got wet to the thigh. He waded to the bow and tied the painter securely to a sturdy sapling at the river's edge. Without a word, he turned back and lifted Annie effortlessly from her seat and set her firmly on dry ground.

"Leave my shoes," Annie called when George went back to retrieve his boots. "I'd rather go barefoot any day than wear shoes."

George sat down and pulled on his shoes and socks before getting to his feet and dusting off the seat of his pants. "Where to from here?" He looked at Peter.

"This way."

Annie followed him through the screen of bushes and saplings, clambering up the rocks, George behind her ready to catch her if she stumbled.

Chapter Four

"Here it is!" Peter stopped by some cedar trees.

"Here's what?" Annie peered around him. The lacy branches of the cedars brushed against the silver grey of the limestone behind them.

"There. The sinkhole." He moved a bit and motioned her forward.

"Oh my, it's deep!" Annie stepped by him and leaned over to look through the branches at the deep depression gouged out of the soft stone.

"Careful." George's fingers dug into her arm. "The edge might not be solid."

She shook him off. "It's fine. I want to see how deep it is." Annie dropped on her belly cushioned by the thick grass and wriggled closer to the edge. "Have you been in there?" She balanced on one elbow and looked back at Peter.

"Sure, lots of times. Me and Tom been here lots. There's all kinds of stuff you can see in the walls. Fish and stuff, leaves…" Peter dropped down beside her.

"I don't think this is such a good idea. You two should get away from there before you fall," George cautioned.

"Don't be such a spoil sport, George. It's safe, honest," Peter replied.

"How did you get down there?" Annie edged closer to the opening. "It looks too far to jump."

"For God's sake don't jump." George sounded like he was about to have an apoplexy.

"Nobody's jumping, there's a rope." Peter got up and rummaged around at the base of one of the cedars. "Me and Tom got some candles and matches and stuff here too. You game?" He raised his eyebrows at Annie.

"Yes! I've never been in a cave before. Can we? You're coming too, aren't you?" Annie looked at George.

"If ye've got yer heart set on it, I guess I'm coming. I can't let you two go off on yer own and maybe get into trouble." The older boy came closer and leaned over to look between the cedar boughs down into the patch of sunlight at the bottom of the hole.

"If we're going, we need to do it now while the sun is still high enough to light up the floor of the cavern," Peter advised. He tied the stout rope to the base of the nearest tree and tossed the end into the hole.

George picked it up and gave a hard pull to test his brother's knot. Taking off his shirt he padded the spot where the rope rubbed on the rocky edge. The play of muscles under the smooth tanned skin of his back fascinated Annie, she found it hard to look at anything else. Peter cleared his throat and elbowed her in the ribs. Heat that was more than the summer sun could account for suffused her body, even the tips of her ears burned. Pete gave her a cocky grin and shook his head.

"Who goes first?" George straightened up and came to stand beside them.

"I'll go, show you how it's done," Peter boasted.

"Then you go, Annie. I'll come down last, so if something goes wrong I'll still be up here to pull you up or go for help," George said.

"Scaredy cat! You're just afraid of a little hole in the ground," Peter taunted his brother.

"Am not! I'm just being careful," he protested.

"C'mon, let's get on with it. We still need to get back up river before someone starts looking for us," Annie urged them.

"Yer right." Peter grasped the rope and disappeared over the edge. In no time, he called up. "Okay, your turn, Annie." His voice echoed hollowly.

Taking a deep breath, she tucked the back hem of her skirts up between her legs and tucked it securely into the belt at the front of her waist, effectively keeping the yards of material out of her way and avoiding the possibility the boy below might see something she'd rather he didn't. "Here goes," she said, biting her lip to try and hide her excitement and anxiety. Her bare feet found purchase on the crumbly stone of the side and she was glad she wasn't wearing the new boots with the slick soles. In less time

49

than she thought it would take, Peter's hands grasped her waist and steadied her until her feet touched the bottom, the sand cool on her bare feet.

"Your turn," Annie called up to George. She looked up, squinting against the light. George's head was backlit by the sun his hair burnished gold, face in shadow.

"Get back out of the way, give me some room."

A small shower of loose dirt and small stones preceded his descent, cascading down to join the debris already on the floor of the hole. Light flared in the gloom outside the sunlit patch of ground directly under the opening above. The candle's flame threw Peter's face into eerie shadow. Annie's breath caught in her throat, it looked like the engraving of Satan in one of Father's books. The resemblance faded when he moved back into the light.

"Here, see the funny wee things embedded in the wall?" He held the candle close to the limestone and pointed to what looked like a big bug.

"How amazing, what is it? Do you know?" Annie leaned so close her nose almost touched the damp stone.

"Nope, not an idea. Some kind of creature that lived long, long time ago. Tom, he knows about these things, he calls 'em fossils." Peter moved the candle and showed her what looked like the imprint of leaves and then a curly something that resembled the top of a turban."

"Who else knows about this place?" Annie whispered, the dark recesses of the sink hole sending sibilant whispers back like ghosts mocking her. Annie shivered.

"Just me and Tom that I know of. We ain't told anybody. This is our special place, a hidey hole if we ever need one, unless maybe your brothers know about it too, like you said." Peter moved further into the shadows. "C'mon, you gotta see this."

Annie moved toward the sound of his voice, aware of George close behind her. The dirt and rocks beneath her feet were damp and a bit slippery. The wavering candle light threw shadows off the rough walls and ceiling.

"Oh my goodness!" She halted so abruptly George ran into her and caught her around the waist to keep from knocking her over. His sharply indrawn breath matched her own gasp. Peter's light revealed rock formations hanging from the ceiling like icicles, shining damply in the cool air. Below the odd creations others rose to meet them from the floor. Annie reached out a hand to touch one. Cold slick wet rock met her questing fingers. George's hand was still warm on her waist and gave her the courage to venture further into the passage after Peter.

Far ahead the sound of rushing water carried to them on the wafts of moving air. "Careful, it's wet further on," Peter called from ahead of them.

"What do you think made this?" Annie wondered.

"The river most likely," George answered. "Look at the way the rock is carved out, it looks like waves."

"It does." Annie was astounded. "Can you imagine what power? It must have taken years."

"I imagine it did," George answered. "Peter, I think we've gone far enough. Come back."

"Oh!" The cry escaped her before she could stop it. Icy water lapped at her ankles.

"Careful, Annie. The last thing we need is for one of us to fall and break something. Petey!"

The light bobbed back toward them and Peter's blond hair came into view, lit from below by candle. "You gotta see this. It's just a few feet more. It's worth it, believe me."

"I don't think it's wise…" George began.

"What is it?" Annie was reluctant for the adventure to end.

"You have to see it," Peter urged her.

Annie followed him for a few feet and around a twist in the passage that cut off any light from the sink hole opening into the upper world. Peter cursed softly and the candle snuffed out. The darkness in the cave was a palpable thing, closing around her throat and smothering the breath in her chest. She opened her mouth to scream but no sound emerged. George grasped her upper arms and pulled her back against him.

"Don't move," he hissed in the stygian blackness. "We can't know where to put our feet. Peter, have you got another light?"

"Aye, just a minute, the matches are damp."

The sharp scritch of match heads striking brought Annie's heart into her throat. Finally, a tiny flame flared and Peter touched it to the wick of a new candle.

"Oh, thank God!" Her hand clutched at her throat.

"Enough, Peter. We need to get out of here," George's voice was thin and sharp as spring ice.

"But, it's right here. You have to see this." He insisted.

"Annie?" George's hold tightened on her arms.

"We might as well see what it is that's got him so excited seeing as we're already here." Curiosity got the better of her fear. Together they moved toward the candle light. Her gaze was drawn downward as they came abreast of Peter.

Mere feet below where she stood water rushed past, appearing and disappearing out of the darkness.

"It's the river!" Peter declared. "Tom says this is how the caves were created."

"What river? The Bonnechere?" Even George sounded impressed.

"The same. You know where the river disappears under the cliffs? Well, Tom says it travels underground through these channels it makes for itself and them tunnels come out again further down."

"How amazing!" Annie bent down to stare at the dark waters swirling by, running so fast it actually had tiny white crests on the waves where it collided with the walls.

"We should go now," Peter said. "This is my last candle." He moved past them and headed back into the smothering darkness.

Annie took one last fascinated look at the water before following him. She glanced up at George, keenly aware of the moisture gleaming off his bare chest. "Hurry," she urged him. "I don't want that candle to run out before we get back to the sink hole."

"I'm right behind you, Annie. Watch your step."

Peter and his candle disappeared around the twist in the passage, for a moment the total blackness descended on her. It was like a physical weight on her skin. George put a hand on her shoulder and it gave her something to cling to in the disorienting dark. The fingers of her hands clutched at the damp slime of the walls, another few steps brought her to the turn in the passage where Peter waited for them.

"You could have waited before the turn." George almost snarled at his brother.

"Oh, sorry." Peter looked startled. "Guess I forgot you didn't have a candle. Me and Tom always have one each."

It was only the work of a few minutes to reach the welcome light at the bottom of the hole. Peter stowed the stub of his candle and the matches in some little cubby. He scrambled up the rope like a monkey and peered down at them. Annie tipped her head back. The opening above her seemed a lot higher than it had from up above. She took hold of the rough rope and pulled herself up a bit. George gave her a boost from below, and she hung for a moment before finding purchase on the rough sides with her feet and struggling toward where Peter waited. When she neared the opening, Peter reached down and helped her the last few feet.

Annie collapsed on the soft grass, flat on her back, chest heaving from her efforts. Above her, the blue sky was shot through with the first pink clouds of late afternoon. She sat up and linked her arms around her knees. George's head emerged from the hole followed by the rest of him. He got to his feet and dusted off his trousers before retrieving his shirt and shrugging into it. The homespun material was smudged with dirt.

Annie rubbed her cold feet wishing she'd brought her shoes and stockings. "We'd best get a move on. It's getting late."

"It took longer in the hole than I thought." George glanced skyward.

Annie hurried along the faint path, branches snagging at her skirts which she'd untucked from her belt. She heaved a sigh of relief when she slid down the bank to the river. George held the boat steady while she clambered in, taking the seat in the stern. Peter settled on the middle seat and unshipped an oar while George untied the painter and pushed off from the shore. He sat beside his brother and took the other oar. Between them the brothers heaved on the oars as the current caught the small craft and tugged it downstream. The boys pulled against the river and slowly made headway back up river.

Not fast enough for Annie. She glanced at the position of sun where it tipped toward the western trees. The family would most likely have noticed her absence by now. Father would be furious, Mother coldly disapproving, she'd feel the rough side of her tongue for sure and probably the bite of Father's belt. Rebellion rose in her, she was sixteen, old enough to be married, or at least walking out with a suitable beau, as Hetty so often pointed out to her. Surely, she was old enough to go off on an innocent adventure. I've done nothing wrong. I spent a lovely afternoon on the river with friends I've known most of my life. She sighed and trailed her hand in the cool water. Father will be sure to make it into something sinful and Hetty will egg him on. And Mother, she never disagrees with Father, ever. But I'm not going to ruin what's left of the afternoon worrying about that. She caught George's eye and gave him a brilliant smile that made him miss a stroke with his oar and earned him a scowl from Peter.

Chapter Five

It took longer to get back to where the little boat had moorings. It seemed the river pushed them back a foot for every two feet they gained. Annie kept a watchful eye on the sun as it swung ever westward in the powder blue sky. Golden light slanted across the land, drawing a vibrant greenness from the trees overhanging the river and lending a surreal cerulean glow to the sky.

At last the small grassy point overhung with trees came into view. Subconsciously, Annie leaned forward as if her actions would lend speed to the vessel. Unease knotted her belly, the heat becoming oppressive again the nearer they came to the moorings. It soured her stomach while her vision danced with the spots brought on by light-headedness.

"Are you well, Annie?" Peter kept his rhythm with the oar while frowning in concern.

"I'm fine, thank you. Just a little warm." She fanned her face with her hand, wishing for the straw hat she'd foolishly left on the bank. The light breeze lifted the heavy hair from her shoulders reminding her of her state of dishabille. Dear Lord, Mother will be distraught if she sees me like this, and Hetty will be sure to egg her on, she never misses an opportunity to paint me as a hoyden. And Father... Well that didn't bear thinking of. She plucked the loose pins from the tangle of her curls, dropping one into the bottom of the boat. Her fingers fumbled as she retrieved it. The trembling was worse while she twisted the recalcitrant tresses into some semblance of a bun, jamming the pins in willy-nilly. At least now it was off her shoulders and could be considered somewhat presentable. As soon as we land I'll find the dratted hat and it should hide the worst of the damage.

The boat nosed in toward the shore and Peter jumped out to pull it all the way in. He took the rope from the bow and secured it to the mooring. George shipped both oars and then stepped out into the calf-deep water. Before Annie could protest, he scooped her up as if she weighed nothing, setting her feet on the grass.

"Thank you," she murmured, the feel of his hands burning through her clothes as if he'd branded her. In spite of the cool shade heat flared through her. He retrieved her boots with the stocking inside and handed them to her.

"Let's get a move on, it's getting late and I need to be back in time for chores. Old man Miller will skin me if I'm late," Peter urged them.

"My hat? I can't find my hat." Annie glanced wildly around the small clearing. "It can't have gone far."

After a quick search it was apparent the hat was nowhere to be found.

"It might have blown into the river?" George suggested. "I can't think what else might have happened to it."

"Oh dear, one more thing I'll have to explain." Annie shoved the pins deeper into her hair, hoping it would stay up. The last thing she wanted was to show up in more disarray than she could help. Taking a moment she shoved damp feet into her boots, tucking her stockings in her skirt pocket.

"Come on!" Peter was already well along the path back to the village.

"We have to go." George took her hand and pulled her along with him.

"Fine!" Annie worried her bottom lip with her teeth, agitated over the reception she might receive from her family, but neglecting to pull her hand from George's grasp. It was a rather enjoyable feeling to have his fingers curled around hers. Safe and comfortable, with a fission of danger. Though what kind of danger she couldn't imagine.

"There they are! We've found them!"

The cry went up as Annie followed George out of the trees unto the back lawn of the General Store. George's fingers tightened on hers for a moment before he released her and stepped away.

"Now, there'll be hell to pay. Begging your pardon, miss." His jaw was clenched, his expression grim.

"It's Annie," she hissed. "And we've done nothing wrong."

George caught her gaze and shook his head. "You know that, and I know that, but do you actually think for an instant anyone else is going to believe that? I can assure you, not your father, and certainly not Mister Miller, or Mister Munroe for that matter." Anger and frustration darkened his eyes.

The group of people descended on them before Annie could form an answer. Peter stopped and turned back to stand beside his brother, stuffing his shaking hands into his pockets. A small figure bolted forward and slammed into Annie so hard it was all she could do to keep her footing. George's hand on her elbow was a welcome support.

"Annie, Annie. I thought you were drownded," Ivan sobbed into her skirts, the battered straw hat clutched in one hand. "I...I..." he hiccupped... "I went down by the river 'cause it was so hot and I found..." his voice broke on a sob. "I found your hat, but I couldn't find you anywhere." Her little brother raised his tear blotched face to stare up at her. "I looked and looked, but you were gone."

"Hush, hush, now. I'm fine, I didn't drown. I didn't even get wet, you silly." Annie stroked his silky hair and wiped away the boy's tears with the edge of her skirt.

"Ivan, quit this silliness. Let go of your sister and come with me." Hetty marched up and pulled the youngster away.

"Annabel Elizabeth Regina Baldwin, you are a disgrace! You have brought shame and ridicule down on your mother and I." Father's fingers bit deep into her arm. The hard set of his jaw and florid complexion didn't bode well for her.

"I'm sorry, Father." She met his gaze squarely. "But, I didn't do anything wrong, we just went for a float down the river, is all."

"No wrong?" Mother's voice rose shrilly. "Taking yourself off with two men of low birth for the whole afternoon?" Her trembling hand held a lacy white handkerchief to her mouth and then dabbed at her eyes. "I don't know how I shall hold my head up in polite company ever again."

"See what you have done, daughter? Not only shamed yourself by your actions, but your mother as well."

The arrival of the Millers and Munroes saved her from digging a deeper hole for herself by offering the defense trembling on the tip of her tongue. Annie looked toward the Richardson boys, Peter's head was drawn down into his shoulders, his eyes on the ground. George met her gaze and something passed between them but Annie wasn't sure exactly what it was. A feeling of solidarity perhaps? Or something more?

"Stop!" The cry was wrested from her as Mister Munroe belted Peter across the shoulders and dragged him away. "George, don't…"

The older boy leaped to his brother's aid but was restrained by Mister Miller who was a bear of a man and easily hampered his attempt. "Nothing more than he deserves, the whelp. And nothing less than you can expect, my lad. Come along, don't make things worse by creating a scene." Surrounded by the Miller clan George was herded away.

"See the trouble you've caused? Not only for yourself but for those orphan boys as well. They can hardly be expected to know better, but you young lady, you certainly know better." Father marched her through the crowd of onlookers, her face flaming with heat that had nothing to do with temperature.

"But Father, it isn't fair…"

"Get in." Father pushed her toward the back of the buckboard. "I don't want to hear another word from you until I give you leave to speak."

Biting her lip Annie settled in the bed of the buckboard and blinked back the tears stinging the back of her eyes. Such a lovely afternoon ruined by suspicious minds. Strong fingers pinched her side and she yelped.

"Do you have any idea what you've done?" Hetty hissed in her ear. "Clarence's mother is making noises about my suitability as his bride, and all because you behaved like a trollop today. What were you thinking running off with those low bred boys? How is Father supposed to find you a suitable husband if you insist on ruining what reputation you have left?"

"Oh do be quiet, Hetty. You're just being horrid," Annie whispered back.

"Horrid am I? How do you think it made Father look today? What with him preaching the Word of the Lord and the need for women to be virtuous and keep themselves pure for marriage. And then you, his own daughter, flaunts her wickedness in front of the whole county. It's you who is horrid and evil." Hetty stuck her nose in the air and joined her mother on the bench seat in front of Annie.

Annie stuck her tongue out at her sister's backside. Beside her Ivan giggled and she shushed him with a wink.

* * *

Later that night, Annie tossed in her narrow bed being careful not to wake Rotha or Alice in the other bed. It was impossible to find a comfortable spot to lie as the cheeks of her bum were tender and hot from the attention of Father's belt. Her face heated with humiliation and anger. She was far too old for him to take the belt to her. The idea of sneaking out of the house and running away turned itself over in her mind. But where would she go and how would she get to wherever it was she decided to go? She had no money of her own and no one in the area would hire her for fear of angering Harold Baldwin, the nearest thing the area had to a doctor and man of God. It was a whole two years until she'd be eighteen, and even then as a

63

woman she had to obey the male whose custody she was in. Be he father, or husband.

Her thoughts drifted to George and Peter. However much Annie felt abused it was probably nothing compared to what the brothers endured. It was a well-known fact Mister Munroe had a violent temper and didn't hesitate to vent his spleen on those unfortunate enough to work for him. Poor Peter didn't even have the option of leaving; he was bound to the Munroes for another three years, regardless of his age. The original agreement between the Munroes and the Barnardo Homes being renewed at the end of the original three years. At least that was what the Munroes claimed, and Annie had no idea how to verify if they were telling the truth. It just didn't seem fair. She'd heard Father talking about it to Mother on the way home, so it seemed that even if Peter came of age he was still stuck with the Munroes. A twinge of pity curled in her stomach. Peter obviously wasn't aware of the fact.

George might fare a little better. Mister Miller was usually a fair man, but there was no way he could turn a blind eye to their escapade. If only to save face in the eyes of the community and Father in particular. Annie thumped the pillow and turned over. We didn't do anything wrong! What is so horrible about three friends going for a row down the river? Why should it matter that she was a girl and her friends were boys? All these pious people certainly were quick to think the worst of an innocent adventure. Minds in the gutter, no matter how Christian they bleated they were. Sleep was a long time in coming, dawn was streaking the eastern sky before she slipped into a fitful slumber.

Chapter Six

July and August moved by in a blur of activity. Annie was kept busy with weeding the large garden, canning vegetables as they became ripe, and collecting berries and fruit and jam making. If she never saw another strawberry it would be too soon. August brought more heat and humidity and no chance to sneak away for a quick dip in the river. If it wasn't Hetty, it was Mother with their eagle eye on her. It seemed every time Annie thought to slip away someone suddenly found a chore that needed doing right this minute.

The wheat and oats were ripening, the long stems rippling in the hot breeze while the heat waves shimmered over the fields. The brilliant greens of early summer merged into the gold and yellow of late August. Father still employed the Richardson brothers to help with the harvest, but Annie was forbidden to even take water or food out to the fields where she was not allowed to go no matter how much her help might be needed. She often caught glimpses of them as she worked in the garden and wished for the opportunity to speak with them. If only to apologize for getting them into hot water. Given the chance Annie would have traded all the enjoyment of the day for the opportunity to have let the boys go off on their own without her. The biggest furor seemed to be because she'd gone off unchaperoned with two males her own age; the boys wouldn't have gotten in nearly as much trouble if she hadn't tagged along.

* * *

Annie shifted the bucket to her other hand and shoved deeper into the brush behind the house. At last she was finally allowed out of sight of the house or the watchful eyes of one of her family. Harvest was over and the chance of her running into either of the Richardsons was negligible. She sang one of her favourite songs to keep herself company and to hopefully scare off any bears that were after the same raspberries and choke cherries Annie was planning to collect. She faltered over some of the words but compensated by humming at the top of her lungs. Reaching the thicket of raspberries she set about collecting the juicy red fruit, popping only a few into her mouth. It was cooler under the trees, but her shirtwaist still stuck to her back and sweat trickled down between her breasts and flies buzzed around her ears. The pail was half full when she stopped to rest. Plunking herself down on a fallen tree near the berry patch, she pushed the bonnet off her head and let it hang by its straps down her back.

She couldn't rest for too long, there was still the mail to fetch from town. Maybe there would be a letter from one of her brothers at the front in Europe. Both men went against their father's wishes and enlisted in the Army soon after Dominion Day. The government had approved conscription which was to come into effect on August 31, 1917. Steve and Evan figured it was better to go on their own than wait to be ordered to enlist. Annie only got to read the censored missive after everyone else except Ivan had seen it. It was hard to decipher the words at times on the often mud streaked paper, and what with the huge blacked out sections which contained information the censors deemed too sensitive, the reading was more an exercise in guesswork than actually reading. Please let Steve and Evan be well, she prayed looking up at the golden streams of sunlight filtering through the green leaves above her.

The war effort had stolen most of the young men and not a few of the young women from the district. The ones who were left were mostly infirm for some reason or another, or deemed too essential to the production of food on the farms at home. Although, to her eyes, there were a good number of malingerers as well. Annie sighed and got to her feet, shaking her skirts out and turning back to the berry patch. One good thing had come of it though; Father quit shoving 'suitable young men' at her. She shuddered at the memory of the oldest Munroe boy. No girl with a brain in her head would consider a union with Jack Munroe; he was a large and loutish as his father and his opinion on 'wifely duties' was well known in the community.

Granted, Father had tried to get some of the more respectable candidates to court her, but Annie rebuffed them, and to be honest, the young men weren't all that keen on the idea either. Jack Munroe had been Father's last ditch effort to get her married off. In a year and nine months she would be eighteen. An old maid to be sure. The idea didn't faze Annie in the least. Better to be an old maid and have at least a little say in her destiny than be the property of a bounder the likes of Jack.

Her fingers plucked the remaining fruit with an economy of motion while her thoughts wandered. It had been weeks since she'd glimpsed either of the Richardson boys. Hetty and Mother had been talking about them, she was sure, but they shut up like a steel trap the minute they realized she was within hearing distance. Still, Annie was certain Hetty mentioned Peter and looked disapproving while doing so. Heavens what could he have done that Hetty would be concerned with? Annie supposed she'd find out eventually, perhaps Mrs. Williams at the Post Office would be willing to share a little gossip? Last time she'd seen Peter was from a distance but he'd looked very thin and if she wasn't mistaken he'd been limping. Surely, old man Munroe couldn't still be angry over what happened on Dominion Day.

A branch snapped sharply on the other side of the wide thicket of brambles. Annie's head shot up and she held her breath, lower lip caught in her teeth. Clutching the bucket in both hands she turned toward the sound as quietly as possible. Nothing out of the ordinary met her gaze. Above her the leaves whispered in the light breeze which blew away from her, bird song and the chuck-chuck of squirrels continued uninterrupted. Convinced she must have been imagining things Annie let out the breath she hadn't realized she was holding and bent to her task again.

"Oh for heaven's sake!" The sharp thorns of the brambles snagged in her sleeve and skirts when she leaned further into the thicket to reach a bunch of elusive raspberries. Yanking herself free she looked up straight into the eyes of a black bear on the other side of the bramble patch. Okay dear, it seems I'm not imagining things. Her lips were numb and the pail rattled in her grasp. Back away, back away. Moving with infinite care, Annie extracted herself from the arching canes and backed away. The bear seemed more interested in cleaning the patch of its bounty than it was in the fact a human was present. Her heart rate kicked up a notch at the appearance of two half-grown cubs waddling out to join the feast. The pulse beating in her ears was so loud Annie was sure the bear could hear it. She swallowed past her dry throat and continued backing away. Once she deemed a safe distance was gained she turned and hurried as fast as her shaking legs would carry her, throwing constant glances over her shoulder.

She burst from the bush onto the grassy verge of Mother's flower garden and paused to catch her breath. Thank goodness the pail of berries was intact, she hadn't managed to spill them in her haste, so at least she wouldn't have to hear the lecture about the need to put preserves up for the coming winter months. Already, the still warm air had the intoxicating edge to it that heralded the beginning of autumn. Annie turned her face to the sunlit sky and let the anxiety flow out of her. It only lasted a moment before she returned to the task at hand. Opening the garden gate she followed the sandy path toward the back door. Nodding heads of blessed thistle and fireweed reminded her of the need to get spade and basket and take care of weeding. Another chore Mother pressed on her in punishment for her foolhardy actions in July. *Wasn't foolhardy at all. It was one of the best days of my life.* Annie frowned at the heavy headed roses Mother favoured, the woman insisted on coddling them along even though they thrived much better in the Ireland of her youth than they did in the back woods of Ontario. *And it's my fingers the thorns prick, not hers,* she thought bitterly.

Reaching the house, Annie pulled open the screen door and entered the kitchen. Bread was rising on the counter, the yeasty scent tantalizing her nose and making her mouth water. Placing the pail of berries on the table she

71

found the canning pot and went to the pump to fill it with water. She set it beside the pail and began the tedious job of cleaning the fruit prior to starting the jam making. Glancing into her pail she wondered if there were enough to indulge in the luxury of a raspberry pie, or maybe some tarts. She sighed in resignation, that would be Mother's decision, not hers at any rate.

"There you are finally," Hetty observed from the door of the hall. "Father wants you to go and fetch the mail. Leave that til later." She waved a hand at the berries.

Annie shrugged and got to her feet. "I need to wash and change my clothes before I go to town."

"See that you don't take all day. Ivan is harnessing Molly and you know how she fusses if she has to stand." Hetty dismissed her sister with haughty flip of her hand.

Annie moved past her and took the stairs to her room two at a time, skirts bundled above her knees. She reached the landing and settled her skirts just as her mother emerged from the front bedroom. "I'm just getting respectable before I go into town for the mail." Annie forestalled the criticism she knew was on the tip of the woman's tongue. Instead Ella Baldwin clicked her tongue in despair at the state of her youngest daughter's clothes.

"How you ever expect to find a suitable arrangement..." she began and then shook her head before continuing past her and down the stairs.

"What if I don't want a 'suitable arrangement'," Annie muttered shoving her door open. It took only a few minutes to tidy herself before she hurried back out. "I coming," she called to Ivan. Pulling the door shut behind her, she crossed the porch and in a most unladylike manner took the three steps in one leap. "Move over," she commanded her little brother who was sitting square in the middle of the buggy seat with the lines clutched in his hands.

"I want to drive." His lip stuck out in rebellion.

"You know Father said you have to wait until you're twelve before you can drive Molly off the farm." Annie moved him over by simply clambering onto the seat and shoving him over, plucking the lines from his hands.

Ivan huffed and crossed his arms over his chest, shoulders hunched in anger. Annie glanced at him out of the corner of her eye, a pang of sympathy rearing its head. The boy was painfully conscientious when it came to his chores, and now that Steve and Evan were overseas fighting the Huns poor Ivan tried valiantly to fill his older brothers' shoes.

"Git up." Annie clucked to the mare and slapped the lines lightly on her rump. The mare snorted and shook her head, making the harness jangle. She expertly turned the horse and buggy and set off down the lane toward the main road.

Turning onto the dirt track, she urged the horse into a jog. Any faster and she feared she'd bounce right off the seat. Father's buggy was better than some but the suspension still left a lot to be desired. Ivan clung to the iron rail on his side and giggled.

Annie had another reason other than speed to keep a brisk pace, the flies were vicious and even Molly was quite happy to hurry as the road ran through the thick bush on either side.

"Can't I drive, please?" Ivan looked at her with the expression that always melted her heart. "Please?"

She hesitated and heaved a sigh. Without slowing the pace, she fixed him a stern glare. "If, and mind I'm saying if, I give you the lines you have to promise not to mention a word of it to anyone. You understand? It'll be me who catches the rough side of Father's tongue and then Mother will have a go at me as well."

"Cross my heart and hope to die." Ivan matched action to word while letting hope enter his expression. "I promise on my life not to say anything to anyone."

"Just until we get in sight of town, okay? I don't need one of those busy bodies putting a bee in Mother's bonnet. Keep her steady and don't get too close to the side or the wheel will get caught in the soft ground." She handed the lines to him, but stayed poised to take them back in an instant if she thought she needed to.

"Thanks, Annie." The smile Ivan turned on her was brilliant.

"Watch the road," she muttered, hiding a smile.

They rattled past Miller's lane and Annie spared a thought for George. She hadn't seen him since they'd passed each other in Eganville, he on one side of the store and she on the other. Annie sighed. Why did the only boy she found even slightly interesting have to be so unsuitable in the eyes of her family? Didn't Father preach it was what a person did with their life that was more important than what station in life they were born to? Of course, that didn't apply to anything or anyone who threatened his exalted position in the community. Fine rhetoric though. Why couldn't people see through the fire and brimstone to the hypocrisy underlying it? Things weren't likely to change any time soon though. Hetty's wedding was coming up soon and surely the Richardson boys would be at the party afterward. Coming as it did at the end of harvest the celebration served a double purpose. The war in Europe was more than beginning to make itself felt even in rural Eastern Ontario. The absence of her older brothers was something Annie felt keenly. She loved them even though the difference in ages meant they never spent much time together.

"Here, give me the lines, Ivan." Annie reached over and reclaimed the leather reins from her little brother. "We're too close to town now."

Ivan relinquished them reluctantly, but without an argument. He waited with the buggy while Annie collected the mail from the General Store and rejoined him. They were home just as the sun dipped into the bushy heads of the maple bush on the hill behind the house. Giving Ivan the mail to deliver to Father, Annie unharnessed Molly, rubbed her down and stored tack and buggy properly before following him into the house.

Chapter Seven

The marriage of Henrietta Clara Baldwin to Clarence Lucas Hiram was the talk of Renfrew County and beyond. Everyone who was anyone was going to be there, along with those of lesser social standing. Annie fussed with her hair one last time, then gave it up for a lost cause and jammed the stupid lacey hat over it. Trust Hetty to insist she wear something that made her look like a cake topper. She grimaced at her reflection in the mirror before turning to the window and looking down into the yard.

Ivan stood at Molly's head looking uncharacteristically spit and polished. Annie grinned when he raised a foot to kick at the dust and then stopped abruptly. Mother or Hetty must have put the fear of God in his young brain. Gathering up her shawl and gloves she left the bedroom and hurried down the stairs. Hetty's shrill voice echoed up the narrow stair case grating on her ear. Taking a deep breath, Annie girded her loins for the ordeal to follow and stepped into the front parlour, as Mother insisted on the room being called.

"There you are! It's about time you put in an appearance instead of lollygagging about upstairs," Mother greeted her.

"I've only just finished dressing, I had to clean up after doing chores," she defended herself.

"No more of your excuses, get on outside. You're to go in the first trip to town and make sure the flowers and the church is in order for when Hetty arrives. Ivan is to go with you, so mind you keep you an eye on the spalpeen."

"Yes, Mother." Annie reached for the door, ready to make her escape.

"Annabelle, do be sure my dear Clarence and his groomsmen have their boutonnières. I just can't have anything amiss. After all, the whole county will be watching us today and we must do Father proud."

Annie paused, hand on the screen door. "Yes, Hetty. Anything else you need me to do?" Her voice was edged with sarcasm which earned her a sharp glance from Mother, but apparently her expression must have been innocent enough because she just waved at her to go.

"Yes, Mother. Yes, Hetty. Anything you say, Hetty. As if a flower is going to make that dry stick Clarence any more appealing," she muttered under her breath, the new boots from July echoing on the boards of the porch. Lifting her skirts, she got into the buggy and settled the material around her, covering as much as possible with a linen sheet. The dust from the road would wreak havoc on the gown.

"Get in, Ivan," she called picking up the lines. "Who else is going in this load?"

"Mother and Father are coming with Hetty, but Rotha and Alice should be with us. Too bad Steve and Evan couldn't be here." Ivan clambered up to perch on the back seat of the buggy.

"Where are they? If we don't get moving we'll all be late." Annie twisted on the seat searching for some sign of her older sisters.

"I'm right here," Rotha said from the shade of the porch swing. "Did Father tell you we're to pick up the Richardson boy to drive the buggy back?" The buggy springs creaked under her weight as Rotha climbed aboard, tucking her skirts around her and covering them with the linen sheet as well. Alice got in as well.

Annie's heart turned in her chest, it almost felt fluttery. She swallowed and pressed a hand to her bodice. "At Miller's or Munroe's."

"Miller's, you silly. Haven't you heard? The other orphan isn't with Munroe's any more. Not after your little escapade." She shot her sister a sideways glance.

Annie swallowed her surprise. "No, I didn't know that. I do hope the boy waiting at the end of the lane, we're late enough as it is. God forbid we don't get the buggy back in time for Hetty to arrive on schedule."

"It is her wedding day, Annabelle. Don't be so mean." Rotha pointedly stuck her nose in the air making Ivan giggle behind them.

Alice maintained her customary silence. Annie sniffed but deigned to reply. Molly picked up her pace in response to the flick of the

79

whip on her haunches. The mid-September air was golden like warm honey pouring through leafy branches overhead. The orange-red tint of the sugar maples glowed in the late morning light heralding the coming of autumn. It was a perfect September day, the sky a deep clear blue and a light breeze stirred the roadside grasses. The liquid notes of the red wing black birds filled the air as the buggy rolled through the low part of the road that bordered the Bonnechere River. The flash of red catching her eye where the birds perched on the brown heads of the bulrushes.

"There he is! Hey, George!" Ivan stood up and waved vigorously, startling both Annie and the horse drawing the buggy.

"Ho, horse. Ivan sit down for heaven's sake!" She settled the mare and glared at her brother. "You know better than that."

"Sorry." Ivan didn't look in the least contrite.

"Good day, Mister Richardson," Rotha greeted the young man waiting with cap in hand. "There's space in the back. Do get in."

Annie avoided looking directly at George though she was dying to find out what happened between his brother and the Munroes. It was the first time since July she'd seen him up close. He had filled out with muscle and he seemed somehow older than she remembered, much more than a couple of months could account for. Somehow today she would find a way to have a few words with him, Annie decided. She peered at him out of the corner of her eye under the pretense of chasing a horse fly from her shoulder.

Her breath caught in her chest. George was dressed in a dark suit, obviously not his own judging by the fit, but none the less giving him an air of sophistication Annie had never seen before. The colour brought out the hazel depths of his grey eyes and emphasized the corded muscle of his thigh. Cheeks heated, Annie turned her attention back to the road ahead, very conscious of her sister's suspicious glance.

She halted the buggy in front of the Lutheran Church. George hopped down and went to stand at Molly's head. Ivan scrambled down and then gallantly offered his hand to Rotha and Alice to aid her decent. Annie folded the linen dust sheet her sister left crumpled on her vacated seat, shook the road dust from her own and folded it neatly. Gathering her cumbersome skirts around her she searched with her boot for the iron step rung on the side of the buggy. It was awkward with one hand on the seat rail and the other attempting to manage her dress. Strong hands clasped her waist and set her gently on the ground. She turned to stare in surprise at George whose hands were still warm on her waist. For a moment words failed her and all she could do was look into his grey eyes and search for something to say.

"Hrrumphhh." Rotha cleared her throat in disapproval and tapped her foot. Ivan stared at them wide-eyed. Annie's heart sank, Lord only knew what he'd tell Mother. Alice merely cocked a disapproving eyebrow at her.

"Thank you," she stammered.

George dropped his hands like she burned him and stepped back. He nodded wordlessly and went to hand the items in the back of the buggy out to the church ladies waiting for the baskets of ribbons and pew bows.

"I believe it's high time you got the buggy back instead of making sheep's eyes at my sister," Rotha declared in a haughty tone.

Annie winced at the disrespect and dismissal in her sister's words. She caught George's eye and gave him an apologetic smile. He shrugged in return as though it was no matter, but his eyes warmed with something Annie couldn't quite put her finger on.

"Annabelle, come on! What are you doing standing there gathering wool? Come inside and at least make yourself useful for a change." Rotha sailed up the shallow steps and through the church doors open to the early afternoon sun. Alice pattered after her.

Ivan scampered on ahead chattering like a chipmunk to anyone who would listen to him. Annie took a step to follow her sister but instead whirled back to speak to George.

"What happened to Peter? Where is he?"

George frowned and glanced over her head toward the dark arch of the church door.

"Annabelle!" Rotha's strident call set Annie's pulse jumping.

"Later, I'll tell you later," George whispered. "Go on, don't make it worse on us."

"Meet me in the orchard under the apples." Annie gathered her skirts and started up the steps.

Rotha grabbed her arm so tight she yelped. "What were you whispering about with that boy? Haven't you caused enough trouble between us and the neighbors? Besides, even you should set your sights higher than the likes of him. He hasn't two pennies to rub together, and you are a Baldwin when all's said and done."

"I was just telling him he must hurry so Hetty won't be kept waiting," Annie lied, crossing her fingers in the folds of her dress.

Her sister sniffed and looked down her long narrow nose. "See that's all it was. You've already cost the Munroes their orphan lad."

"What do you mean? And let go of me!" She twisted her arm free of the painful grip, glaring at her sister while rubbing feeling back into her forearm.

"Now isn't the time. Go see what Ivan is up to and make sure those women are placing the pew bows properly according to Mother and Hetty's instructions. Go on, git." Rotha gave her a shove.

Rather than argue further, Annie stepped into the dim interior stopping to let her eyes adjust to the light. The familiar scent of lemon and beeswax filled her nostrils. Moving down the centre aisle she pretended to inspect the bows and nosegays attached to the ends of the pews. It all looked fine to her, and besides once Hetty was on her way down the aisle there was no way she was going to stop and make a scene. The scene would come later if she was displeased about anything, but by that time Annie would have made herself scarce. She grinned and went to help the church ladies with the final touches.

* * *

Long tables set under the maples and chestnuts by the side lawn overlooking Mother's rose garden strained under the weight of the wedding feast. Annie tied an apron over her good dress and tucked her rebellious hair behind her ears. Dratted stuff would never stay up in a bun no matter how many pins she shoved in it. Although Father declared the celebration would be a dry one, Annie knew there was a keg or two of beer behind the barn and a barrel of whiskey in the wood shed. She giggled, Father would have kittens if he found out, but it would give him something to give out about in his hell and brimstone sermon on Sunday.

Ivan was employed to stand by the food and wave a pine branch to deter the flies. A number of the younger neighbor boys were likewise at work. Good then, one less thing to worry about. Until they get bored. The lead crystal punch bowl shot rainbow light over the short grass and up into the leafy canopy where the red-gold rays of the setting sun caught the faceted glass. She grimaced, Lord help anyone who harmed Mother's prized bowl or treated it with less than the respect it deserved. The delicate bowl had made the long trip from Ireland by ship along with her newlywed parents years before. Annie crossed her fingers, as long as it wasn't her and she was nowhere in the vicinity if disaster struck, it would be fine.

The newly wedded couple was holding court on the raised boards of the front porch. Hetty looked happy and apprehensive at the same time. Annie supposed her sister was thinking of the marriage bed she was obliged to go to later that night. From what she'd seen in the barnyard when her menfolk thought she wasn't looking, the whole thing seemed to consist of the male animal mounting the female from behind with a lot of grunting and sometimes screaming in the case of the barn cats. For the life of her Annie couldn't see why any woman would want to subject herself to that. But Mother insisted it was a wifely duty and no matter how distasteful it was, it was also something that must be endured for the sake of the babies that would result.

Yech! I think I'll just stay an old maid. There are worse things, I'm sure. Pausing for a moment in the shade of the big maple Annie considered the man her sister had married and shook her head. There was nothing about him with his weak chin and skinny shanks that would induce her to take her clothes off in front of him let alone allow him to touch her private places. Well, Hetty's made her bed so she'll have to lie in it, I suppose. May she find joy of it.

No one seemed to need her to do anything at the moment so Annie leaned on the rough trunk behind her and allowed herself to relax. Her gaze wandered over the milling guests. Twilight turned the sky to deep blue violet, some of the older boys were carefully lighting the lanterns and torches set around the lawn to provide illumination as night fell. The first stars glimmered overhead and over the cedar swamp in the hollow beyond the bottom hayfield the fireflies blinked in a crazy dance to music only they could hear. Her gaze lighted on Alice, blonde and willowy, ladling out punch. Her shy sister was leaving for Ireland the day after tomorrow to live with Father's relatives and teach school.

Speaking of music, she straightened up from the tree, the fiddler was tightening his bow and Joe's squeezebox emitted squawks and wheezes. Annie loved the eclectic combination of the local musicians and was grateful Father had been unable to hire the string quartet from Ottawa that Mother and Hetty had their hearts set on. Stuff and nonsense, and such a waste of money when money and other things were so scarce due to the war in Europe.

I wonder where George is. He said he was coming, but maybe something came up...I really need to find out what happened to Peter.

Nothing horrible, I hope… She'd have to look for him later by the apple trees, but for now it was time to clear the picked over remains of the wedding feast. Father was getting ready to start speechifying, she could tell by the way he straightened his coat and pulled on his lapels. Annie wouldn't be needed for any of that and she might as well get a start on the clearing up and bring water in for the dishes. She glanced around for Ivan and his friends but of course they were long gone, off on some adventure of their own no doubt.

She was glad to escape the long winded speeches and declarations of the bride's admirable attributes. There was a cauldron of warm water simmering on the stove in the summer kitchen which she used to fill the wash basin. Thankfully someone had thought to fill it and set it to warm so she didn't have to lug heavy pails from the well and wait for it to boil and then cool enough to stick her hands in.

Wrapping the left overs in waxed brown paper she piled the perishables into a woven basket and carried them out to the ice house. It was full dark by now and the rear of the house was lit only by the stars and half-moon riding low in the sky. Laughter and voices from the front and side of the house spilled into the blessed silence where she stood. Sighing she wiped her hands on the now soiled apron and turned back to the kitchen to start on the dishes. She'd finished two tubs of dishes and emptied the dirty water out onto the vegetables in the root garden near the back door. The table was still piled with pans and silverware.

Somewhere nearby the whippoorwill called. Annie glanced at the waiting dishes and then pulled off the apron and flung it over a chair. The night was still warm but there was an edge to the breeze that said it was closer to autumn than mid-summer. Snatching a shawl from the hooks behind the door, Annie slipped out into the darkness. She needed no light to show her the way to the orchard, her feet found the familiar path without faltering. Underneath the trees the night deepened, she glanced upward at the stars shining through the lacy branches. Such a perfect night. Now if only George was waiting for her by the apple trees...

Annie slowed near the old gnarled trunks. When she was younger this was her favourite place to play. The Apple Tree Man was her secret, one she never told anyone about. She spent many happy hours playing in the shade of the largest tree, climbing into the spreading arms and dreaming the long summer afternoons away. The evening breeze picked up flicking at the fringe of her shawl. Tightening her grip on the material she reached out to trail her fingers along the rough bark.

"Hello, Apple Tree Man," she said and laughed at her own foolishness.

"Annie?" A figure disengaged itself from the shifting shadows.

"Oh! My, I didn't see you there. George, is that you?" Annie took a step back, just in case she needed to beat a hasty retreat. The last thing she wanted was to run into one of the guests who were in their cups.

"It's me, Annie. I was beginning to think you weren't coming." George moved out of the darkness into the small patch of pale moonlight between the trees.

"It took longer than I planned to get free, and I had the chores to tend to," she replied, holding her breath and daring to move closer to him.

"I'm right glad you came," he sounded a bit breathless.

"Me, too. I've hardly even seen you since…well…you know…"

"Did you get in much trouble?"

George started to wander between the rows of trees and Annie followed in silent accord. The cricket chorus was background music to the rustle of leaves in the breeze and the call of the whippoorwills. The night wrapped them in black velvet lighting their way over the grass glistening with dew in the starlight. A million thoughts whirled in Annie's head but she was loath to break the silence and shatter the spell that seemed to have enthralled her. George's shoulder brushed against her for a moment and her heart skipped a beat and breath caught in her throat. She glanced up at him to find him smiling at her, teeth shining in the faint light, an enigmatic expression on his earnest face. Annie found herself smiling in return and when he took her hand she didn't hesitate or pull away. It seemed the most natural thing in the world to stroll through the abandoned orchard while the stars wheeled overhead.

They reached the edge of the bush and halted. Enchanted evening or not, there was no way Annie was going to go walking in the bush at night. Not without a shotgun and a lantern at any rate, and then only if the cows had gotten out again.

George pulled her down beside him on a fallen tree, not relinquishing his hold on her hand. Her fingers twined with his, she tipped her face up to look at him. His features were in shadow and he suddenly looked like a stranger to her. A thrill of fear speared down her spine, the night suddenly filled with danger.

"Annie," he whispered, raising a hand to touch her cheek. His voice dispelled the sensation of strangeness replacing it with another emotion altogether.

She covered his hand with hers, fingertips finding the rough calluses on his workman's hands. "What happened to Peter?" Annie uttered the first thing that came to mind, anything to distract her from the excitement gathering in her belly that she somehow knew her parents wouldn't approve of. Though she couldn't have told why she thought that.

George's expression changed and he dropped his hand from her face. Though he still held her fingers in his, she felt he had withdrawn from her even though the warmth of his thigh still penetrated her skirts.

"What is it? What happened?" Any other emotion was forgotten in the face of her companion's obvious distress. "Was it my fault? Because of what we did on Dominion Day?" She freed a hand from his grip and pressed it to her throat.

"Aye, in a way, I guess it was. 'Twas the straw that broke the camel's back at any rate." He paused and stared out into the shadowy orchard where the trees threw faint images across the wet grass.

"Was Mister Munroe awful mean to him? Oh, I couldn't bear it if he was beaten because of me."

"It weren't the first time he got his arse scalped and it weren't the last. Munroe always seemed to be looking for a reason to lay into him, and nothing I could do to stop it." George's fist clenched on his thigh, impulsively she laid her hand over it and squeezed.

"What happened, George? You can tell me, I won't breathe a word to anyone. Cross my heart and hope to die." Annie suited action to words.

A grim smile twisted his lips. "Weren't your fault. If anything 'twas mine. I should have known better, should have thought about the consequences. Instead all I could think of was spending time with you." He bit his lip as if he'd said more than he intended to.

"I wanted to spend time with you too, so that makes me responsible too," she confessed.

The boy beside her fell silent for so long Annie feared he wasn't going to tell her where Peter was and what happened to him. Morbid thoughts chased around her head and she was more than half afraid to hear the truth of the matter. What if he was dead? Or maimed?

"Peter's gone."

The flat finality of the words startled her so she almost slipped off the log.

"What?"

"He's gone. My little brother's gone, again. We got separated in the foundling home in Liverpool. I got shipped to Canada and thought I'd never see him again, but somehow God arranged for Peter to get shipped here too and placed near enough we could see each other. Now he's gone again..." His voice broke and moisture glistened on his cheek.

Annie moved without thinking and cupped his face in her hands. "Tell me what happened, George. Let me share your burden, help you if I can." He pressed his cheek against her hand and blinked.

"Peter's gone and joined up. Went to the Recruitment Office in Eganville and volunteered. Nothing Munro could do to stop him what with Petey supporting the war effort and all."

"Why would he do that? I mean, he didn't have to, being a farm labourer and all. Father tried to keep Steve and Evan home but they were bound to go. From the letters they send it doesn't sound like being in Belgium is a bowl of cherries. It's hard to tell, what with the censor's black marks all over the paper."

"He went because he couldn't stand staying another minute at Munroes. The old man about beat the skin off him and he vowed he'd not go back. But you know our situation, we got nothing but the clothes on our backs and those we're beholden to our masters for everything. There was nowhere for him to go and no money to get there if there were a place." George's faced twisted bitterly.

"But surely, there was money set aside from the work he did, I mean he did the work to cover his keep at Munroes, but then he worked all over the county too—"

"And not a penny of it do we see, Annie. We're nothing more than rented mules and not as valuable as all that."

"But, he's safe right? Is he in Toronto, or Kingston? Where did they send him…" Annie faltered at the bleak look on her companion's face. Her hands fell to her lap where she clasped them together.

"He's overseas. Near as I can figure he's in France somewheres. I haven't had a letter from him yet, just the one right after he enlisted and told me he was getting on a troopship to London and then on to France."

"Oh my stars! You must be worried sick."

"I am that. I'm his older brother, dammit." He smote the log with his fist. "Begging your pardon for my language." George tipped his head in her direction. "I should be able to protect him and there's nothing I can do. I feel so…useless!"

"I can't even begin to imagine," Annie found herself saying. "It would be like Ivan going to war. I don't think I could stand it."

"Well and all, it doesn't seem I have any choice but to stand it," his voice was grim.

Annie was at a loss for words and the silence stretched between them like an overtight elastic band. An owl hooted in the maple trees and she started to her feet, heart racing. "How silly of me," she gasped and made to sit back down.

"No, it's far past time we were going back." His words kept her on her feet. "Someone will no doubt be looking for you by this time." A frown creased his brow.

"Probably not, they'll be far too busy arranging the chivary and planning mischief. I don't want to go back yet, it's so peaceful here." She boldly reached out took his hand, when he didn't protest Annie led him back into the orchard, smiling at the tracks they left in the dew wet grasses.

"What are you going to do? Are you planning on volunteering as well?" She tilted her head up at him.

"Can't. I'm still tied to the Miller's. I promised I'd stay for another six months. I can't in all honour break my word. It's about all I've got, that and what little pride I have left."

"So, you'll be around? We can still see each other once in a while?" Annie quivered at the forwardness of her words. Mother would have kittens if she ever found out her youngest daughter had been so bold, and with someone so far below her social standing. She snorted and kicked at a mushroom. Social standing be damned! George is far nicer than those fellows Father wants me to walk out with. It's my life. I should be able to do what I want!

"What are you snorting at, Annie?" George's expression lightened and the beginnings of a real smile twitched at the corners of his lips.

"Nothing, really. Just all this silliness about not marrying beneath yourself and damned if you actually even like the person they want you to spend the rest of your life with." She paused and swung his hand gently. "You never answered me. We can still see each other can't we?"

"I'd like nothing better, surely you know that." The intense look on his face set her heart racing and heat flooding her body. "But I can't see how. Mister Baldwin would pin my hide to barn door if he caught me sniffing around his daughter."

"Well, he doesn't have to know, does he?"

"What?" George stopped walking and turned to look down at her.

"With Steve and Evan gone, I have to go bring the cows in out of the bottom field every morning and night for milking. I'd be missed if I loitered in the morning, but in the evening it's just me doing the milking and shutting up the chickens, sheep, and pigs. It's usually just coming dark by the time I'm finished. If you can get away, meet me by the big stand of pines on the bank above the cedar swamp. The cows generally go that way for some reason. It wouldn't be for long, but at least I could see you and know you were doing okay. What do you say?" She tipped her head back and to her dismay the last of the pins slipped from her hair which cascaded over her shoulders.

George caught his bottom lip in his teeth and reached a tentative hand to smooth the shining blonde strands back from her face. "It's risky. More for you than me. I have no reputation to speak of, you on the other hand, have a lot more to lose. Your Father is correct, you know. No decent man will have you if your reputation is lost." Starlight gleamed in his grey eyes.

"Are you not a decent man, then?" Annie whispered and leaned closer to him, one hand coming to rest on the rough material of his shirt. His heart thumped under her fingertips, drumming as fast as her own.

"It's fire we're playing with, Annie," his voice went husky and he cleared his throat.

"Aren't you a decent man?" she repeated. "Would you not have me, reputation or no?"

"We shouldn't do this. It isn't right and it isn't fair. To me or to you." George took both her hands in his and set her away from him. Raising their joined hands he kissed her knuckles, the rough hair of his moustache tickling her fingers.

"Will you meet me in the evenings when you can?" she persisted, running her tongue over her dry lips. Her gaze riveted to the column of his throat where it rose out of his open collar. His Adam's apple bobbed when he swallowed.

"God help me, I will, Annie," he whispered.

Without another word he led her back to the edge of the orchard, pausing in the last of the shadows. She opened her mouth to speak but he laid a finger over her lips and shook his head. "'Tis better this way." He kissed her fingers before releasing her hands. "I will come when I can, but it won't be every night," he cautioned.

Annie glanced down at her clasped hands, the imprint of his mouth burning her skin. When she looked up a moment later she was alone.

Chapter Eight

The low winter sun bathed the snow in a red-orange glow and touched the bare trees with gold. Annie's breath puffed out before her as she struggled to wade through the knee deep snow. Where were those blasted cows? She'd searched all their usual haunts when they managed to knock down the cedar rail snake fence. Today they'd simply walked over the top of it where this afternoon's wind piled the drift high and hard enough to make easy passage.

She glanced at the sun. If they didn't miraculously appear soon she'd have to leave them. Father would be livid, but there was no way Annie wished to be caught in the wintery bush after sunset. The moon was full and the chorus of hunting wolves had serenaded her for the past two nights while she lay with the quilts pulled up to her nose in bed.

Sighing, she stopped on the edge of the gully where the small creek lay frozen below. No sign of the five cows she was searching for. Thank heavens for small mercies the bull was in the barn and so she wasn't also dealing with his fractious nature. Most of the time the animal was quite tractable for her, but in the bush with his harem…? Annie shook her head. Quit woolgathering, girl. Or you will be wolf bait.

She let go of the trunk of the maple sapling she was using to balance and stepped back. The wind changed and she froze. Is that them? Is that Sally's bell?

The evening wind carried the distinct, but faint, clang of a cow bell. Annie frowned, they never headed east when they went on a ramble, especially in the winter. Setting her jaw, she turned her footsteps toward the sound. Now she'd found a trace of the missing animals she couldn't very well in all good faith head for home. Although that was exactly what her frozen fingers and toes were urging her to do. Wrapping the scarf tighter around her neck and lower face she set off.

A branch sprang back at her and slapped her cold cheek. Uttering words which would earn her a beating if Father ever heard her, Annie blinked back the sting of tears and plowed on. If only Steve and Evan were home she wouldn't be out in the rapidly darkening woods on her own. Ivan was helping search but only closer to the house. Why couldn't the stupid war in Europe just end? Annie missed her brothers more than she ever thought she would and not just because they made her lot in life easier. She forced herself to keep moving, distracting herself with thoughts of the war and her brothers. Evan's last letter had the return address of a convalescent home, he said he was fine but had come down with the influenza that seemed to be running rampant through the wet muddy trenches in Belgium and France. Some associates of Father's in London had sent some newspapers with their last post. Of course they made the whole affair seem much more glory filled than it was, but Father said if you read between the lines and what they weren't saying you could determine a great deal.

A loud moo startled Annie so she nearly tripped and landed on her bum. Only by grasping a young birch sapling did she manage to avoid falling. However, the tree did dump its small load of snow on her head. Yelping, she jumped back and beat the wet snow from her coat and scarf. The light was fading and the bush was full of deepening shadow. The cow mooed again and she turned in that direction. In a few minutes she came across the track the silly things had beaten in the snow. Moving quicker on the easier going Annie called for the herd. If she was lucky they would be cold and hungry and quite tired of their adventure and happy to come to a familiar voice. Only Sally and Maud were still milking, but their udders should be making their demands made by now too. Another point in Annie's favour.

Shoving through some serviceberry bushes she emerged into a bit of a clearing. Releasing a sigh of relief at the sight of all five missing bovines, she spread her arms and began herding them back toward the barnyard. The sun was mostly behind the trees and low hills but there was still enough light in the sky for her to determine which way was home. A long shivering howl rose into the clear royal blue heavens which was answered by another and then another.

"C'mon, girls. Get moving unless you'd rather be somebody's dinner." She waved her arms and the cattle obligingly moved off toward home. Annie smiled, their sense of direction when it came to food and home was probably more finally honed than her own. Although, left on their own they would have stayed where they were waiting for someone to come find them and urge them home.

"Need some help?" George's voice sounded from the deep shadow just to the right of the trail.

"George? Is that you?" Annie couldn't keep the breathlessness sound from her voice. "You scared the life out of me," she declared coming even with him. "How did you know where to find me?"

"Ivan told me which way you were planning to go." He fell into step beside her, the cows moving ahead of them at a quicker pace now.

"You went to the house? Was that wise?" She frowned at him.

"Just by luck Mister Miller sent me with a message for your father. It was fairly late when I arrived and Ivan was just coming in from the bush. Mister Baldwin was worried for you and I volunteered to go out and look for you. Your mother didn't want him out in the dark with that cold he has."

"Well, I'm glad it was you who found me. Go on, git up there, girls," she interrupted herself to urge the cows on.

"I'm happy to hear that." George took her mittened hand in his.

"You must be frozen! Where are your mitts?" Annie was aghast to see his hand was bare.

"Don't have any, I'm afraid." He shrugged.

"Why, that ridiculous! Surely the Millers can spare you a pair of mitts!"

"Not so far, but the winter's young yet. It's just the end of November."

Annie stopped in her tracks digging in the big pockets of her coat. She pulled out a pair of thick hand knit mittens and shoved them at him. "Here, they're a bit tattered, but they're warm."

"No, now. They're yours, I can't just take them." George shook his head.

She ducked her head. "I made them myself. It would please me if you would wear them."

"In that case, how can I refuse," he replied gallantly and pulled the mitts over his reddened hands.

"Oh, I can see the lights of the house. We're almost home. You must come in and get warm," Annie insisted. The cows broke into a shambling trot at the scent of home and scrambled back over the drift and broken fence into the barn yard.

George halted and caught her hands again. "I mustn't. Mister Miller was expecting me back some time ago. I still have chores to do there."

She tipped her head back to see his face better in the strengthening moonlight. "You won't be in any trouble will you? For being late, I mean?"

"I would for sure, except your father was kind enough to write me a note explaining he asked me to go and look for his lost cows. No, that should set things right." He paused and leaned down to brush her cheek with his. "You go on in the house, I'll lock the cows in the barn and throw them some hay. I have permission to borrow a lantern for the walk home. Go on." George released her hands and gave her a gentle push. "I'll be fine. Don't worry."

"You will be careful? And be sure to take a full lantern."

He nodded and moved toward the barn.

"Good night then, George," she called softly.

"Good night, Annie." His voice floated back to her through the moonlit shadows.

* * *

With one thing and another, the next time Annie had a chance to speak to George was at Christmastime. Father held a huge prayer meeting on Christmas Eve and everyone who was able was expected to attend. Annie made herself scarce and slipped into the back of the room once everyone had taken their seats. She found a place with the people standing along the wall at the back. Mother would complain Annie was just being contrary by not sitting with the family and the other social elite of the county. She sniffed at the notion and grinned. The corners of the room were cast in shadows though Mother had candles set everywhere along with the lamps and the ornate cranberry glass chandelier which had made the journey from Ireland with her parents. Annie hated the thing, although she had to admit it was beautiful all lit up. It was an absolute pain to keep clean and dusted and that chore fell on her shoulders. So even though she could admire the rosy glow, tomorrow evening would be spent cleaning the soot from the glass, polishing the fittings and filling the reservoir with new lamp oil.

She felt George's presence behind her before his hand touched her shoulder. Keeping her expression neutral and not looking, she took a half a step back so she fit against his side. When his arm slipped around her waist she covered his hand with hers. In the shadows she was sure no one could notice.

"Happy Christmas." His breath tickled her ear and stirred the tendrils of hair at her temple.

"Happy Christmas, George." Her fingers tightened on his. It seemed somehow sacrilegious to experience the feelings racing through her body while Father preached abstinence and fire and brimstone. Somehow the man could even make a joyous occasion like

Christmas bleak and full of sin. Annie allowed herself to press a little closer to George's side and hide a giggle at his reaction. God forbid she be caught smiling at meeting.

"You shouldn't do that," George whispered even while he drew her closer, his thigh pressing against the back of her legs.

In answer she rested the back of her head against him. "Why ever not?" she teased boldly though it felt like she was playing with a fire she didn't quite understand the volatility of.

"We need to talk later. Alone." He pulled away from her though his hands lingered on her waist for a moment longer.

Annie glanced at him feeling lost and bereft without the warmth of his nearness. Darn it, now she'd gone and ruined everything. She hadn't done anything more and considerable less, than those girls in the dime store novels she had hidden under her mattress. Reaching blindly in the shadows she sought his hand. "I'm sorry," she whispered. "Please don't be angry with me."

Work roughened fingers closed over hers for a brief second before he released her. "Later," he repeated and moved further away from her.

Humiliated and angry, Annie sniffed deeply through her nose like Mother did when she was deeply vexed about something. Well, if that was the way of it, then fine. Served her right for throwing herself at his head like that. He must think I'm a light skirt. No well brought up young lady acts like that. Haven't I heard that often enough? What was it Evan and Steve used to say about that girl in town? Why buy the cow if you can get the milk for free, that's it. I never understood what milking a cow had to do with anything, but I think maybe I'm beginning to see what they were talking about. Dear God! How humiliating to be talked about like that. I wonder if she knows. Oh of course she must. Maybe she doesn't care? But I do! I'll just find George Richardson later and set him straight.

Clenching her fists in the folds of her dress Annie turned her attention to Father's sermon, glad the dim light hid the angry spots burning on her cheeks.

Once the preaching part of the meeting was done with Annie was kept busy with making sure the refreshment table was well stocked and the punch bowl never ran dry. Mother had hired a couple of the girls from town to help out and even now one of them was plucking the big tom turkey in preparation for tomorrow's supper. It was a chore Annie didn't envy her in the least. It was well past eleven-thirty by the time she had a minute to herself. There was a brief lull and she plunked down on the top step by the landing, hoping she was far enough out of the lamp light that no one would notice her. Her feet hurt in the high button boots and she wished she could just take them off and pad around in stocking feet. No chance of that though. Leaning her head against the railing she closed her eyes and let the tinkling of Mother's fingers on the piano in the parlour wash over her. Some were singing

106

carols, and one or two people were hopelessly off key. It shouldn't matter though, should it? It was Christmastime and people were supposed to be kind and generous.

"Found you. I wondered where you'd gone off to." A waft of air warned her of his presence before George perched on the stair beside her.

"What did I do to make you angry?" Annie opened her eyes and looked over at him, her earlier anger forgotten.

"I'm not angry with you, Annabelle. Indeed, quite the opposite." He trailed a finger down the curve of her cheek.

"Oh." She sat up straight and caught his hand in hers, twining her fingers around his. "Then why did you act like you were. And why are you calling me Annabelle?" Bewilderment made her frown and produced an uneasy sensation in her stomach.

"Because what I need to talk to you about is important to me so it seemed like I should use your proper name." His hand tightened and he moved a hair closer so his thigh touched her.

"Whatever could be so important? You're scaring me, George."

"Oh, no. No reason to be afraid, I promise you." He paused and swallowed hard.

Annie leaned closer, catching the sweet scent of punch on his breath, along with something else. "Have you been drinking?" She narrowed her eyes. "Who brought drink into this house?"

"Some of the boys have something in the woodshed, and I only had one swallow. For courage…and luck…" His voice trailed off.

"Why should you need courage, or luck for that matter?" Annie was totally confused now. "Did something happen to Peter? Did you hear from overseas?"

George shook his head. "Annie, surely you know how I feel about you?"

"I think so," she answered slowly.

"I'm hoping you feel the same about me…I mean you seem to…like being around me…and we're friends, aren't we?"

"Exactly what do you mean…feel the same about you? I'm not sure how you feel about me…it's not like we've ever talked…about…about our feelings…" She trailed off while his hands tightened on hers.

"That's what I'm trying to do right now, but you're not helping me much."

Annie huffed a breath and regarded him seriously for a long moment. "Right then. Why don't you start by telling me how you feel about me? Then I can tell you if I feel something similar. How's that for a start?"

George swallowed loudly and closed his eyes for a second. "It's a place to start," he sounded unsure.

"Go on, then," she encouraged him controlling a surge of impatience.

"This is hard, Annie. Harder than I thought it would be. You must have guessed how I feel about you. We've been friends for years, but this is more...don't you think so too?" His expression was tense and earnest and his vulnerability wrung her heart.

"More than what?" Annie whispered. "Are you saying you'd like to be more than friends? Like walking out together?" She held her breath, sure George could hear the thunder of her heart, feel the excitement in the pulse throbbing in her fingers.

"Would you be agreeable to that?" His hands clenched on her fingers.

"I think I would like that very much." Annie nodded in agreement. "Very much."

"Really?" George drew back to see her face better. "You're sure? What will your parents think...I know I have nothing to offer you at the moment, but I have a plan."

"I'll be eighteen soon enough, so although Mother and Father will likely not be thrilled I haven't chosen one of the suitors they deem acceptable, they're terrified I'll die an old maid," she declared.

"But they can make things hard for you, you're still living under their roof. It might be better to keep our understanding a secret for now. At least until I have the means to support you and a roof to put over your head."

Annie considered his words for a long moment. He's most likely correct about Mother and Father pitching a fit, and I do have to live with them. Oh, why couldn't I have gone to Trenton with Rotha to work for the British Chemical Company in the munitions factory?

Her letters were peppered with exciting words like TNT and cordite that Annie had to look up in Father's dictionary. However, she lived with a bunch of girls from the factory and seemed to have lots of fun even with the long hours she worked. Father was concerned, Annie remembered, because Rotha mentioned her skin was turning a pale yellow, but she wasn't worried because girls who had been there far longer than her were a brighter yellow and doing just fine. Father muttered to Mother about liver damage and toxicity, but he hadn't followed through on his threat to go and collect her. Thinking of Rotha brought up thoughts of Alice who, if her letters were any indication, was thoroughly enjoying her post in County Dromore, Ireland

"Annie? What are you thinking? You're a million miles away," George interrupted her thoughts.

"Sorry, yes." She pushed Rotha and Alice to the back of her mind. "It would be easier to keep this between us, at least until we're in a position to do something about it. You mentioned a plan, what is it?" Annie moved closer to him and leaned her head on his shoulder. His arm came up around her and she sighed with pure happiness.

Resting his cheek on her hair George began to lay out his plan. "I've convinced Mister Miller to release me from my promise—"

"That's wonderful!" Annie straightened up to smile at him.

"There's a catch, but not one I'm in disagreement with."

"What catch?" This couldn't be good.

George took a deep breath and then plunged on. "I'm enlisting in the army. I leave first thing in the new year. I've already talked to the recruitment office and Mister Wilcock says they'll be glad to have me."

"You're enlisting?" Annie felt faint, a weird buzzing rang in her ears. "But here, in the reserve. You're not going overseas, right?" This could not be happening, not on the happiest day of her life.

"No, I'm volunteering for active duty. I'll be part of the Canadian Infantry, the Eastern Ontario Regiment. I've already signed up actually." He paused and looked a bit sheepish. "I should have said that right up front and not beat around the bush like I did. I passed the medical so I'm just waiting for the call up. I'm a private in the 21st Battalion, Canadian Overseas Expeditionary Force," he finished proudly.

"Oh George!" Annie buried her face in her hands to hide her fears.

Gentle hands took her shoulders and pulled her against his hard chest. His arm encircled her and one hand stroked her hair. "I'll have a regular pay packet, Annie. A way to save money for our future. I don't have any other prospects and to tell the truth I feel like a heel staying here at home when fellows are over there fighting the Huns. For God's sake, my little brother is over there in France."

Annie forced herself to calm her expression and sat up a bit but kept close to his side, head on his shoulder. "Have you heard from Peter? He's safe isn't he?" She was proud her voice didn't shake.

The chest under her hand heaved with a deep sigh. "Last letter I got was from a convalescent hospital. He came down with a bad case of the influenza, just like one of your brothers. From what I could decipher around the censor's black-outs a lot of the lads are down with it. The letter took ages to reach me so he must be back with his unit by now. He said he got a Good Conduct Badge for something he did in one of the skirmishes. Oh, and he thinks he's going to get attached to the Canadian Railway Troops as a sapper. That'll mean an increase in pay for him."

"I'm glad he's better, but not that he'll have to go back to the front. I'm sure it's not as glorious as the newspapers make it out to be. Father says it must be cold and wet and muddy from what he knows of the weather in France."

"He's probably not far off the mark, but the censors black out any reference to stuff like that, and any mention of where they are or where they might be headed. I'm surprised they let the bit about Pete joining the Railway Troops through."

"What's a sapper, by the way? I don't imagine it has anything to do with trees and maple syrup." Annie was glad to see she made George smile.

112

"No, nothing to do with maple trees. Although he'd be a sight safer if it was." George's face clouded with worry again.

"Peter's a smart lad, he can take care of himself," Annie comforted him. "But what does he do?"

"Pete said he had to complete the Engineer DP1 training—"

"So, he's an engineer now? Isn't that something! What does DP1 stand for?"

"It's training he had to complete in order to become a sapper."

"Do you know what a sapper does?" Annie was filled with a sense of pride for the serious youth she had known before he went off overseas.

"Not exactly, but he does a lot of technical things now. I'm right proud of my little brother. He helps build bridges, does some combat driving, tactical breaching of enemy targets, getting rid of explosive ordnance and they go ahead of the troops and make things ready for them to advance. Setting up living quarters and preparing roads and rail lines for the troops to advance."

"But, isn't that more dangerous than actually fighting in the trenches? You mean they actually go ahead of the army toward the Germans with no back up support?" Her stomach was in knots again.

"From what I understand that's the gist of it. Pete seems to love the building and he says he's learning all sorts of useful things. He

113

doesn't say anything about it being dangerous, but I bet he's scared lots of the time."

"You're...you're not going to get involved with that are you? Be a sapper, I mean?" Annie shivered in spite of herself.

"I might, if I get the chance. If I could get in the same company as Pete I could keep an eye on him. See to it he stays safe." His eyes took on a cold steely look in the dim light of the landing.

"Just see that you stay safe and come back to me." Annie pressed against him and was surprised to feel his body tremble.

"Lord, Annie. I love you so much it hurts. I wish we could get married before I leave, but I know we can't. Promise you'll wait for me? Promise?"

"I promise, George. I'll wait for you as long as it takes. Maybe this stupid war will be over by the spring and all the boys can come home safe and sound." She hesitated and gathered her courage. "I...I love you too," she whispered.

Her breath whooshed out of her. Strong arms pulled her tight to his body and his mouth sought and found hers. The sensation was unlike anything she'd ever experienced. Every nerve ending in her body seemed to be on fire and a need she couldn't identify flared in her belly, swelled her breasts where they pushed against his chest.

"Oh my," she exclaimed when he broke the kiss. "Oh my."

"Annabelle! Where have you gotten to?" Mother's voice echoed up the stair well. Her footsteps moved toward the kitchen.

George stood and drew her up with him, holding her tight while they balanced on the top step. She turned her face up for his kiss and was disappointed when he only pressed his lips to hers briefly. She opened her mouth to protest but he forestalled her.

"No, Annie. If I keep kissing you I won't be able to stop, and I won't compromise you. Not when I can't offer you anything right now. There'll never be another girl for me. You're sure you want to wait for me? I'll understand if you don't or you change your mind when you think on it some." He looked so miserable, her heart turned over.

"Of course, I'll wait for you. And I won't change my mind. I've got to go down," she said at the sound of footsteps in the hall at the foot of the stairs. "It must be midnight by now and Mother will need me to help settle those who are staying over. You wait here and come down after I've gone and the coast is clear." She stood on tiptoe and kissed him, unable to leave him without one more kiss. "I love you," she declared, gathered her skirts, smoothed her hair and descended the steps.

"Oh, there you are. What have you been doing, you look like a hoyden?" Mother's eyes narrowed with suspicion.

"I went up to my room to lie down for a moment. I wasn't feeling well, but I'm fine now." She drew her mother away from the stairwell. "What do you need me to do? How many are staying over?"

"Not that many, thank goodness. I don't know why your father insists on a late night before Christmas Day. The boys are bedding down out in the hayloft, it's not so cold out that they'll freeze. Drag the pallets out of storage and get fresh linens from the press. Set them up in the front parlour and make sure the fire will last the night. Don't put any little ones near the stove, mind." Mother hurried off still muttering to herself.

Annie started when George ghosted by her with a light touch to her waist and a secret smile just for her.

Chapter Nine

Christmas Day was a blur of noise and colour and, for Annie, chockablock full of work. There was no time to steal even a precious minute with George. It was hard not to keep searching for him with her eyes. The few times their eyes met it was like an unspoken communication passed between them and filled her with happiness. Annie had never felt anything like this before and was at sixes and sevens to know how to deal with her emotions.

Finally, the festivities were over and the guests were preparing to leave. Father was talking to the Millers in the front hall while George waited a respectful distance behind them. Annie took the opportunity to be near him with the excuse of fetching him his coat and hat. She was inordinately pleased to see the mitts she'd given him sticking out of the pockets. Her fingers lingered on his as she passed him the coat and she thrilled at the light in his eyes as he took the garment. The spell of intimacy was broken by Father slapping Mister Miller on the back and wishing him Happy Christmas and a prosperous New Year. Her ears burned with rage earlier when she overheard her father complimenting Mister Miller on his charitable nature for including the 'English orphan'.

Pompous, both of them. It's Christmas for heaven's sake, it shouldn't be about what the neighbors think, but about being kind.

Annie hid her flushed face and hurried to gather the wraps of the next set of departing guests. Her head was full of plans to see George before he left in January. George, her fiancé. The thought gave her a queer feeling, as if she were embarking on a great adventure with no idea what to expect. There was no one she could talk to about it. Even if she confided in one of her girlfriends somehow it would get out and it was too new and precious to spoil by sharing it with someone other than George.

* * *

The weather took a turn for the worse sometime in the early hours of Boxing Day. The blizzard lasted almost a full five days and the drifts were piled so high on the fields and the roads that travel was impossible. Annie spent more hours than she cared to count out in the wind and snow shovelling paths to the barn, the pig pen, the chicken and sheep house and the well. The water in the buckets froze quickly and it was almost a full time job keeping them free of ice. Father finally moved the pigs and sheep into the barn. They herded them along the narrow cleared path with no incident. Annie and Mother bundled the chickens up and took them to the barn as well. With the loft still full of fragrant hay and the heat the cows and horses threw off the water buckets only had a skim of ice to break. Annie smiled at the chickens making themselves at home roosting on the stall partitions and scratching in the straw.

She sighed, finding eggs in the morning would be a chore, but at least the silly things wouldn't freeze where they sat. Her thoughts were never far from George and as the days ticked by the possibility of seeing him before he went to the train became slimmer and slimmer. In the privacy of her room, hers alone now that Rotha was in Trenton and Alice gone off to Ireland, she replayed every moment of that magical night on the landing. She smiled every time she crossed the landing and started downstairs. If she closed her eyes and tried hard enough she could actually see him sitting there waiting for her.

The new year of 1917 came and went with no letup of the cold and snowy conditions. Annie fretted at the deep drifts that kept the family isolated from news. The only information came by word of mouth from those brave or desperate enough to slog through the weather to reach medical help. Father was still the only person a lot of locals trusted to administer to their bodily needs.

There was no word from George and Annie sometimes worried the things she remembered from Christmas Eve were just a sugar plum dream conjured up by her imagination. But late at night, tucked warmly in bed when by rights she should have been asleep, she replayed the innocent caresses and kisses, especially the kisses, and knew it was real.

* * *

The weather finally broke in mid-January. Thank goodness for the January thaw, Annie thought while the eaves dripped the melting snow that would transform into rainbow icicles as night fell. Of course, it also meant the darn snow melted into slush making sloppy going when she went about her chores. Wet snow and mud clung to the hem of her skirts and found its way through the seams of her work boots. Bother, she would have to rub them with sheep grease tonight even if they wouldn't be quite dry after evening chores. If she left them too near the kitchen stove the leather would crack, but otherwise the interior would still be damp and cold come morning.

Muttering, she sidestepped to avoid a small icy lake lying in the middle of the barn yard. A faint 'hallo' carried on the wind causing her to whirl around and look toward the end of the snowy lane. The sun reflected off the blanket of white setting her eyes to watering. She blinked to clear them and raised a mittened hand to shade her face. Yes, there was a small figure, black against the heaped drifts, fighting its way toward the house. Chores forgotten for the moment, Annie gathered her sodden skirts and hurried back to the house.

"Someone's coming!" She closed the door behind her to keep the heat in and shucked her snowy boots in the small mud room off the kitchen. "Mother, Father! Company coming up the lane," she called into the interior of the house. From the study came the sound of a book closing sharply and then Father's footsteps as he crossed to the front door. Annie glanced at her filthy hems and shrugged. It was most likely someone come to see about a medical ailment or to see if Father could come out to a patient too sick to come themselves. Warming her hands at the stove for a minute to thaw her fingers, she filled the kettle and set it to boil. No matter what the purpose of the visit, a pot of tea and biscuits would be in order. Annie smiled. Mother refused to acknowledge she was no longer living in the high society of Dublin, every visitor no matter how ragged was offered tea and biscuits and polite conversation if they were so inclined. If any one came expecting a tot of whiskey to warm them they were sadly mistaken. Father was a teetotaller and refused to have drink in the house. She wondered if he guessed about Steve and Evan's now neglected stash under the floor boards of the wood shed.

The thought of her brothers made her think about the war and that made her think about George and Peter. Her pulse quickened, maybe the caller came from town and had thought to bring the mail and Father's much anticipated newspapers. Maybe there would be word from George, a note left for her at Arlo's, if not a real letter. There wouldn't have been enough time for a letter to get to her, even if it was just coming from Valcartier in Quebec. She paused in the act of pouring boiling water into the tea pot to warm it. Imagine, George is in Quebec! It must be so exciting to see all those new places. Why, I've never been farther than Renfrew or Killaloe. I wonder does he have to speak French? I would be so lost, Father insisted I learn a bit of Latin, but French?

"Annie, I declare I don't know what is wrong with you?" Mother hurried into the room her shoes tapping impatiently on the wood floor. "Quit your woolgathering and wet the tea." Shaking her head and throwing her daughter speaking looks, Ella Baldwin bustled about taking down the good cups and saucers and setting out the biscuits reserved for special guests on a dainty Irish linen doily on the cake plate. "Bring the tea in when it's ready." She stopped in the doorway, cake plate in hand and took in Annie's dishabille, eyes narrowing in exasperation. "Never mind, do get cleaned up and then join us in the parlour."

Annie blinked at her mother's back disappearing through the door into the hall. Me? Why ever do they want me in the parlour? Oh, Lord don't let it be bad news. Her hand shook so the hot water spilled from the tea pot onto the counter. She threw a dish towel over the puddle and swished the remaining water around the china pot before dumping it into the slop bucket. Setting the now warmed teapot on the counter she reached for the tea caddy. Measuring the correct amount she added it to the delicate china pot followed by the boiling water. The knitted tea cosy looked oddly cheerful when she drew it over the pot and left the tea on the table for Mother to collect. The murmur of voices came from the half-closed door of the parlour and she was sorely tempted to listen for a minute. Instead, she gathered her heavy skirts and took the stairs two at a time. Annie shimmied out of the skirts and underskirts, leaving them in a puddle on the floor before changing her stockings and pulling on a clean but serviceable brown skirt and blouse. After all, once the business with the visitor was done she still had chores to attend to.

Annie gave her hair a lick and a promise, shoving the hairpins back into her bun. There was nothing she could do about the tendrils drifting around her temples right now so she would have to do.

Rather than bound down the steps in the way that made her mother sigh, Annie went slow, taking the time to compose herself for whatever lay ahead. She paused at the parlour door and rapped with a knuckle. Father insisted on his privacy and she would never dream of entering a room he was in without permission.

"Come, Annabelle," he ordered.

She pushed the door open and stepped in. Mister Miller sat in the Morris chair opposite Father by the fire. Mother was perched on the love seat, the tea tray before her. Annie halted, her heart in her throat. What is Mister Miller doing here? Fear sent the blood rushing from her head. Did he find out about me and George somehow? How could he? George would never have said anything.

"Annabelle, where are your manners?" Father frowned at her.

"Hello, Mister Miller." Annie dropped a tiny curtsey, just like Mother insisted was proper.

"Good day to you, Miss Baldwin." He smiled at her, blue eyes twinkling. "You're far to grown up a young lady now for me to call you by your Christian name."

"Come sit down, child." Father waved her further into the room, indicating she take a seat by her mother.

Annie was grateful her skirt hid the fact her knees were trembling. She glanced at her mother in inquiry and received a faint shrug in reply. So Mother has no idea what is going on either. The knowledge did nothing to calm her nerves. I wonder where Ivan is.

Father leaned forward and set his tea on the small occasional table between the two men. "So tell me, Seth. What brings you all the way out here with the roads in this condition?"

The humour in Seth Miller's eyes faded and he glanced at Ella. "I finally managed to get into town this morning and Arlo asked if I'd mind collecting your mail." He indicated the waxed leather satchel leaning against the chair leg.

"Your London papers are there and some letters…"

"That was very kind of you, Seth—"

The other man held up a hand to forestall him. "There's something else and I agree with Arlo it couldn't wait."

Mother gripped Annie's hand so tight it hurt, her other hand pressed to her throat. Annie glanced at her, her own heart thundering in her ears so she could hardly hear the two men. Seth Miller reached into an inner pocket of his coat and pulled out something that crackled like folded paper. "This came a week ago, but the roads have been impassable or Arlo would have found some way to get it to you sooner." He handed the folded paper to Father. Annie looked on fascinated, like being enthralled by the cold dark stare of a serpent.

Carefully, Father unfolded the telegram. For she could see it was a telegram now. Black spots clouded her vision and she realized she was holding her breath. Mother drew in a quivering breath and squeezed Annie's hand so her nails bit into the flesh. Father's eyes moved as he scanned the brief message and then passed his hand over his eyes.

"What is it, Harold. For God's sake tell me." Mother's words were choked as if her throat was too narrow to allow them to pass.

"It's Steve," he said, eyes still on the yellow paper in his hand. "He's been reported Missing In Action."

"When, when was it?" Annie was amazed she could speak.

"November. In France, near some place called Ancre. In the Somme, I believe," Father's voice was emotionless.

"I'm sorry to bring such bad news." Seth cleared his throat. "There's still hope of course, Missing in Action means he could be in hospital somewhere unable to say who he is."

"Or he could be dead. Oh my poor baby." Mother dissolved in tears on Annie's shoulder.

"Mister Miller's right, isn't he, Father? You know the papers are full of stories about fellows people thought were dead suddenly reappearing. If he was gassed maybe he can't talk..." She patted her mother's back awkwardly. It was so unlike the woman to display any emotion at all, let alone in front of male company.

Father roused himself and seemed to notice his wife's distress for the first time. "Take your mother upstairs, Annabelle. She's had a shock. Get her to lie down and I'll be up with a potion to calm her shortly."

"Yes, Father." The last thing Annie wanted to do was leave before she found out all there was to know about Steve, but Father had dismissed her and there was no point in arguing. Besides Mother was likely to weep herself into a faint if she kept up the way she was. "Come, Mother. Wouldn't you like to lie down for a bit?" She stood and pulled the woman up with her. "Good day, Mister Miller," she said before guiding her out of the room and up the stairs. It was strange to be in her parent's room. Annie couldn't remember if she'd ever been further than the threshold. She helped Mother lay down and got a cold cloth for her face, wringing it out in the basin by the window. Cold fingers closed over hers when she laid the compress over Mother's eyes.

"Thank you, Annabelle. You're a good girl," she whispered before her hand dropped to the counterpane.

Stunned Annie stared at the supine woman. It the kindest thing she could ever remember her mother saying to her. That fact scared her more than the contents of the telegram.

Chapter Ten

Leaving Mother resting, or at least not weeping now, Annie bolted down the steps hoping to garner more news of her brother. She skidded to a halt at the bottom and smoothed her skirts, tucking a recalcitrant curl behind her ear. Father and Seth Miller stood in the parlour door. Both men looked up at the sound of her footsteps on the hall floor.

"Annabelle, please see Mister Miller to the door, if you will. I must write to your sisters." He paused, his chest expanding with a deep sigh. "And Evan, I suppose. Though Lord only knows how long it will take to reach him. Please find Ivan and break the news to him, your mother is in no state to speak to the boy." Father shook hands with his guest and disappeared into his den.

Annie cleared her throat and led the way to the front door, Seth Miller following behind. She retrieved his coat from the hall tree and held it out to him. Relived of the heavy weight she gathered up the still damp scarf and mitts. In a matter of moments she dug through the container of heavy knitted woolen mitts kept by the front door and produced some dry hand coverings which she handed over.

"Yours are still damp and it's far too cold to be going out with wet mitts." She added a long scarf to the offerings.

"Thank you, Miss Baldwin." Mister Miller accepted the items and glanced over his shoulder down the hall. "I have something for you." His voice was almost a whisper.

"For me?" Annie took a step back in surprise.

"Yes, hush my dear. Keep your voice down. It's from George. I promised I would get this to you but the opportunity hasn't presented itself until now. I am sorry it coincides with the bad news from France." He pressed a small parcel wrapped in worn calico into her hand. "I think it best if your parents don't know where you got this from, or indeed that you are in possession of it at all." His eyes twinkled with humour. "If I understood George correctly the token is in the way of a promise made and an understanding."

Annie clutched the package in shaking fingers, her heart too full for her to speak. She nodded, blinking back the tears stinging the back of her eyes.

"He's a good lad, for all that he's an orphan without two pennies to rub together." He patted her arm. "You could do far worse, my dear." Mister Miller took a step back and raised his voice. "I must be off while the daylight holds. Good day to you, Miss Baldwin. Harold," he spoke over her head.

"Seth, and thank you for coming all this way to bring us news of Steve." Father emerged from his study.

Annie shoved the small parcel into her skirt pocket and closed the door behind the visitor. She turned to find Father regarding her with an odd expression on his face.

"What were you discussing with our guest? I was surprised to hear voices in the front hall when he should have been on his way long ago."

"Nothing of any consequence, Father. His outer garments were still damp so I looked up some replacements for him. It didn't seem neighbourly to send him out into the weather without warm clothing. Especially after he came all this way to bring us news of Steve." Her voice caught on her brother's name. Please, Lord, let him be safe.

"Very well. It was kind of the man to come out in these temperatures. Go check on your mother and then I believe you still have chores to finish." He dismissed her and closed the study door behind him.

Mother appeared to be sleeping when Annie peeked in the door. She slipped into her own room and changed into warmer clothes and added an extra pair of stockings before going down to the back mud room. She paused in the hall and then collected the tea tray from the parlour. Depositing them on the counter in the kitchen she tidied things a bit. It was vexing the girl who usually did the more menial house chores wasn't able to come on a regular basis in the winter months. The extra chores fell to Annie, of course. She grimaced. Oh well, the dishes could wait, as could her muddy clothes still on the floor of her room, the stock could not.

Her fingers brushed the hard knot of the secret gift in her skirt pocket. Excitement mixed with some other intangible feeling rushed over her. George, a gift from George. A promise Mister Miller said. Whatever can it be? Nothing stolen, I hope. He has no money… The thought was hardly formed before she dismissed it and felt ashamed for even entertaining the idea in the first place. George was nothing if not honourable, he was a good man.

The cold hit her like a fist and she pulled the door shut behind her and slogged down the barely broken path through the snow to the barn. Inside it was marginally warmer and at least out of the wind.

"Where have you been?" Ivan leaned on the pitchfork behind Molly's straight stall next to the milk cows. "The chores are almost done and I'm half froze."

"Mister Miller came to call and I had to play maid for Mother." She paused and swallowed. There was no easy way to break the news, but that didn't make it any more palatable to be the one to tell him. "Ivan, put down the fork and come here for a minute."

"Why?" Her brother frowned at her. "Chores ain't gonna get done by themselves."

"Aren't, Ivan. Chores aren't going to get done by themselves. Father would skin you for speaking like one of the hired men. Chores'll wait for a moment." Annie sat down on an over turned bucket.

Ivan leaned the fork against the oat bin and crossed the straw strewn floor to join her, upturning another bucket to sit on. "So what's so important?" He twisted a bit of timothy hay between his fingers, shredding the seed head.

"Mister Miller brought the mail from Arlo's and a telegram," Annie hesitated and then rushed on, "it's—"

"It's Evan, isn't it? He's dead," Ivan's voice was dull and lifeless.

"No, not Evan. It's Steve…he's been reported missing in action. So there's a very good chance he's alive and just wounded…"

"Stop it, Annie." Ivan looked up an expression of dread and a far too adult knowing on his young face. "I know what it's like over there, the mud and the rats and the…and the…killing…"

"How could you possibly know any of that? It's just your over active imagination. I'm sure it's not as bad as all that."

The look he levelled at her chilled Annie's heart. "I read the papers. Dug 'em out of the trash before they got burned, and I read Evan's last letter when Father didn't know. I can read between the lines, suss out what the censors blacked out. It's hell on earth, Annie. Don't let anyone tell you any different." Ivan swiped a

132

hand across his face and went back to shredding hay.

"I know it is, Ivan. I was hoping you would be spared that knowing. We have to keep positive thoughts though. As far as we know, Evan is safe and for all we know Steve is as well."

"Safe? Safe? How can you call sleeping in mud and filth with shells falling everywhere safe? Not to mention running into enemy fire and getting caught in razor wire..." his voice choked off.

"You didn't read that in the papers. Where did you get that information?" Annie narrowed her eyes at his bowed head.

"Sammy," he whispered. "Sammy's brother came home with no leg and blinded by the mustard gas. I saw him just before the snow started. Sammy says he scared the heck out of him waking up in the night screaming and crying and clawing at his face. The fire popped, you know how pine pops sometimes, and Mathew turned white as a sheet and dragged his mother under the table, babbling about taking cover and dirty Huns the whole time. I didn't stay too long after that."

"I'm so sorry you saw that. And I'm sorry for Mathew as well. I heard he was invalided out, but Mother wouldn't tell me anything more about it."

"So don't tell me Evan is safe, or that Steve might be alive, you hear me!" Ivan surged to his feet, hands fisted on his hips, glaring down at

133

her. "If I was old enough I'd enlist and go over to beat those dirty Huns. Pay them back for all the trouble they've caused." He glared down at her.

"I feel like that too, Ivan. But then I got to thinking that most of those German soldiers are probably just as young and scared as ours are. They're just following orders and trying not to get killed themselves."

"You're defending those bastards that are killing our boys?" Ivan's voice rose in shock.

Annie sighed. "Mind your language, Ivan!" Her tone softened. "That's not what I'm saying, although I dare say most folks around here would agree with you. Let's forget I said anything and concentrate on thinking good thoughts for our Steve and Evan, shall we?"

Ivan snorted and with a final glare at his sister crossed the floor and snatched up the pitchfork. He stabbed the pile of half-frozen manure viciously with the tines before depositing a chunk in the manure sled. Annie ignored his angry muttering and set about forking hay into the cows. Once her hands warmed up, she slipped off her mitts and started the milking. The small bump in her skirt pocket reminded her she still needed to open George's gift. Oh, George, please be all right, please come home to me. Lord keep them all safe, Evan, Steve, George, Peter...all the Eganville boys.

Ivan was still shooting her dark looks by the time chores were finished. Annie

134

extinguished the lantern, making sure it was fully out, before following her brother into the early evening dusk. The sun had dipped behind the trees though light still leaked into the clear sky. She set the heavy milk pails down in order to shoot the bolt on the barn door. Pinpricks of stars held back the curtains of the night, glimmering in the royal blue sky. Sighing, she picked up the covered milk pails and trudged toward the house. They would need to settle for a bit before the cream could be skimmed off.

When Annie entered the kitchen she was relieved to find Mother tending the stew pot. Father's potion must be working as the woman seemed composed if unusually quiet. Ivan shed his clothes in the mud room and disappeared up to his room. Annie envied him, she worked just as hard, if not harder than he did, but because he was a boy her brother was exempt from 'womanly duties'. She smothered a snort.

* * *

By the time Annie could retire to the privacy of her cold room it was late. She set the calico packet on her bed and changed quickly, pulling on two pairs of woolen stockings and a thick sweater over her flannel nightgown. The fire in the room's small fireplace was reduced to barely warm embers. She padded over and poked at it with a long stick. Leaning over she blew on the embers till they glowed brighter, then she added more kindling and made a tripod of some hardwood over the growing flame. Once she was sure it was well and truly caught, she lit the lamp by her bed with a spill and then slid the bed warmer she'd retrieved from the fireplace between the sheets. Her clothes from earlier in the day hung by hooks on the wall, once they thawed and dried enough Annie would knock the worst of the mud and dirt from them. With luck they would be serviceable enough to wear again. Washing laundry in winter was particularly onerous.

She climbed into bed, snuggling her stocking feet by the warming pan. Her hand shook from more than the cold when she picked up George's gift. Her fiancé, she smiled and hugged the thought to her heart. With fumbling fingers she untied the string and unfolded the thin cloth.

"Oh my!" The lamp light glimmered on the mother of pearl face of the ladies wrist watch nestled in her palm. "It's beautiful. I wonder where ever he could have gotten this." Her fingers stroked the band which was inlaid with mother of pearl as well. The smooth patina of the watch told her it had been worn often and well taken care of. She lifted it from the wrapping and laid it across her wrist. A small square of folded paper fell onto the quilt. Setting the time piece aside she unfolded the note. George's handwriting sprawled across the page.

Dearest Annie,

I had hoped to give this to you in person, but circumstances have made this impossible. I have entrusted Mr. Miller with the task of delivering this safely into your hands. It is the only thing of value I have and it is my dearest wish that you accept it as a token of my love and a seal of our understanding. In case you are wondering, this watch belonged to my mother and is the only thing of hers we managed to hang on to. I have spoken with Peter about giving it to you and my brother in is full agreement that you should have it. As you may have guessed, Peter is quite fond of you, I daresay nearly as fond as myself. I will make every effort to write to you, but the mail is very inconsistent from the front, as I have experienced trying to keep contact with Peter. As of this writing, as far as I am aware, he is well and hale. I fear I must close now, I must leave in time to meet the train.

With all my good wishes,

George

At first she thought it was a smudge of ink, or a trick of the light, but on closer inspection she saw he had contrived to add a tiny x and o at the end of his name. She touched a finger to it while tears stung her eyes and burned in the back of her nose. Please keep him safe, dear Lord. I know it's selfish of me, but please let him come home safe and sound. Annie picked up the watch and fastened it on her wrist. What was George's mother like? Was she pretty, or worn out with having babies and trying to raise them without proper funds? From the little the brothers had revealed to her, the family had not been wealthy. Their father worked as a platelayer, a drayman, and a carter. They'd lived in someplace called Wavertree, Lancashire which was part of some city called Liverpool. George told her his mother died soon after Peter was born and he really didn't have a clear memory of her being only two when she died. George and Peter ended up in the Liverpool Sheltering Home when their father proved unable to cope with the loss of his wife and taking care of young children. Neither George nor Peter knew what had become of their older brothers Alfie and Jim.

The snap of the fire broke Annie's train of thought. She got up shivering and banked the flame so it would hopefully last the night, barring a gust of wind swooping down the chimney. Back, snuggled under the blankets she turned on her side and fell asleep cradling the watch to her cheek.

Chapter Eleven

Spring of 1917 came late. The roads muddy and almost impassable well into the first week of May. Annie closed the trunk holding the last of her belongings and looked around the now bare room. She crossed to the curtainless window and gazed out over the familiar fields. This was the only home she'd ever known and now Father decreed they were moving house. Mother seemed excited by the prospect of being near Hetty again. Annie was not so enthralled at the idea. She wasn't even sure where it was they were going to. Some small place near Georgian Bay called Sprucedale. The place was much smaller than Eganville from what she could gather from her parent's conversation. The letter to George crackled in her bodice when she bent down to secure the strap around the trunk that would safeguard the latches from coming open during transit. It was securely locked, but accidents could and did happen enroute if Mother's paranoia was to be believed.

As a precaution Annie had managed to speak privately with Mister Miller when he came to make his farewells of the family. He promised to let George know where she was if her letter somehow went astray and he came back to the area searching for her once the war

139

was over. Please let that be soon. How much longer can this misery go on? Letters from George were few and far between arriving tattered and water stained at irregular intervals. Annie cherished each thin sheet, tucking them securely in the bottom of her small purse not trusting them out of her possession even momentarily.

So far Mother and Father didn't seem to be aware of her correspondence or perhaps they were aware and didn't disapprove. Her mouth twisted in a parody of a smile. The latter situation wasn't a likely possibility. More likely they just hadn't bothered to pay any attention to her affairs, which suited Annie just fine, thank you. Now Hetty, she was another story. Her older sister would be all over it like flies on a dead hog. She'd have to go canny once they were settled in their new home and Hetty once again was a frequent visitor.

Taking the corn broom, she gave the floor a last lick and a promise, letting her thoughts wander at bit. Hetty was nigh on a year married now and still no sign of babies. Granted her husband was a bit of dry stick, but still one would think he would expect his marital rights, whatever they were. Mother carried on about them and the onerous duties involved but Annie had never quite figured out exactly what those duties entailed. Nothing messy or Hetty would have kittens and scream blue murder, she was sure. Giggling, Annie left her trunk in the middle of the empty floor for the men Father

140

hired to help them move and began to sweep the upper hall. She faltered by her older brothers' bedroom door. What if Steve comes home and finds us all gone? What if he can't find us again? What if he thinks we've deserted him, if he's maimed he might think we don't want anything to do with him? Panic closed her throat and her lungs refused to take in air. Annie leaned on the wall and forced herself to breathe. This is silly. I've got to stop acting like a loon. Someone will tell him where we are and offer assistance if Steve needs it. We've good neighbours hereabouts. I know Father wrote to Evan so the letter will catch up to him eventually. Shaking her head, she finished sweeping and took the broom downstairs to see what else needed doing at the last minute.

Annie took one last look around the familiar barn yard and the surrounding bush. She'd taken the time last night to go out to the spot where she used to meet George. If he came home and found her and her family gone she'd taken the precaution of hiding a note in sheltered hollow branch on the old maple. The missive was wrapped in waxed canvas to keep out any wet. George would know where to look for it as they'd used the hiding place to communicate in the past.

"Annabelle, hurry up!" Father called from the buggy where Mother and Ivan were already seated.

Giving Molly a stroke as she passed, Annie climbed up and scrunched in beside Ivan. The big work horses in the pasture whinnied as Molly trotted by. Father sold the livestock with the farm, even Molly would be remaining. One of Arlo's boys would return her to the farm and unharness her once the Baldwin's unloaded the buggy in Golden Lake at the train station. Annie's heart was sore at losing the amiable mare and the other livestock. She hid her upset because Father would frown on any emotional display and Mother would sniff and look down her aristocratic nose at her youngest daughter in dismay. Ivan bounced on the seat beside her when they detoured into Eganville and stopped at the general store to pick up Arlo's son. He cheerfully wedged himself in beside Ivan after politely greeting Annie's parents. Annie took a deep breath to ease the tightness in her chest when the Golden Lake station came into view after a long and uncomfortable ride. It was really happening; she was leaving the only place she'd ever known. Annie wished she could feel even a tiny bit of the excitement Ivan was displaying. Instead she swallowed back the thickness in her throat and willed the panic rising in her gut to still.

Molly halted by the station and Father helped Mother down. Ivan leaped over the side and set about helping the Arlo boy unload the trunks. Annie clambered down unaided and stood uncertainly at the edge of the platform while her parents oversaw the transfer of their personal effects to the baggage car. She took the opportunity to slip around the far side of the

142

buggy and give Molly one last hug, all she could do was hope the new people would be good to her, and the work horses. The square building squatted between East and West bound tracks, the platform so close to the tracks only a few feet separated the distance between.

"Annabelle!" Mother's imperious summons sent her scurrying back to the station porch. "There you are, come along now." She sailed on ahead, head held high as if she owned the place. Annie trailed along behind, tucking her wayward hair back into her bonnet.

The small station was fairly empty. The trains carried mostly lumber and other cargo with only a few passenger cars. Mother settled on an upholstered bench and surveyed the room much like a queen would survey her domain. Annie always found her attitude somewhat embarrassing and failed to emulate it. She went to the door and watched the back of the buggy and Molly disappear back toward Eganville. Father and Ivan's boots echoed on the planks of the station porch. Twisting her small finger purse in her hands Annie started in surprise. Paper crackled in the reticule where none should have been. Hiding her puzzlement she started toward the far side of the station.

"Where are you going, Annie?" Ivan tugged at her skirt. "Father says we need to stay close, the train will be here soon. Aren't you excited? We're going on a train!"

"I need to use the rest room. Tell Mother I'll only be a moment." She hurried toward the outhouse by the far door of the station. Once inside the small odiferous confines she pulled open the crocheted strings of the small pouch. Nestled inside was a thin paper envelope. "How in the name of all that's holy did that get there?" she whispered. The purse hadn't been out of her possession…except when I dropped it in the buggy and Frank Arlo picked it up for me. Her fingers rattled the paper as she unfolded it. George! It's from George. Bless Mister Arlo, the letter must have come recently and hadn't had a chance to make its way out to the house. Her eyes scanned the awkwardly written words.

Dear Annie,

I am well, or as well as one can be in this situation. I have escaped the influenza that has stricken my regiment. The news is uncertain, but I did get word of Peter, though I have no idea how old that news may be. He is recovered from the bout of flu and sent back to his battalion. He is now attached to the <words were blacked out here> and is now a <more words blacked out but Annie thought she made out the word 'sapper'>. He was gassed and spent some days in <blacked out> convalescent home but is now apparently back in action. I pray for his safety.

I hope this finds you well and in good spirits. I see no end to this conflict and wish I could be back with you walking through the bush and listening to the whippoorwill in the evening as the sun sets.

Hoping to hear from you as soon as the mails can bring me your words.

Best Regards,

Pte. George Richardson

Canadian Infantry (Eastern Ontario Regiment)

21st Btn

"Oh my, George." Annie crushed the letter to her breast and blinked back tears. Poor Peter, catching the influenza and then getting gassed, how horrid. A flash of shame lanced through her at the thought that at least George was safe.

Shoving the thin paper back into her reticule she composed her features and re-joined her family just as the whistle of the approaching train split the air. Then it was all a flurry of following Mother, having her ticket checked and getting into the passenger car. She sat beside her mother who motioned her to take the window seat, Mother having no interest in the scenery. Ivan and Father took the seats facing them. Mother tutted about the condition of the car, much too dusty and unkept for her liking even though it was the best money could buy.

Annie shifted the small finger purse on her lap, strangely comforted by the faint crackle inside. This was her first ride on a steam train, or any train for that matter. While she wasn't as over the moon about it as her younger brother, it was certainly an exciting experience.

* * *

The novelty of riding on a train wore thin fairly quickly. The seats were uncomfortable and she was forced to shift her weight often to ease the numbness in her bottom. The train slowed as it climbed the Algonquin Highlands, newly minted spring leaves met her gaze as the engine strained onward. The early morning frost had burned off now and the sun picked out flashes of colour in the bush. Beds of white trilliums lay scattered under the edge of the trees; bright yellow coltsfoot waved their heads in the ditches beside the tracks. Chokecherry, wild apples and raspberry brambles reared snowy heads while the birch tossed pale green catkins against the vivid blue of the spring sky. Their forward movement slowed further allowing Annie to press her face to the window and admire the delicate purple and yellow violets massed in the damp low places by the tracks. The windows did open, but remained closed to keep out the smoke and dirt. Eventually she tired of staring at the passing scenery and glanced at her mother who was studiously reading her Bible verses. Father caught her eye and fixed her with a stern stare. Sighing, Annie dug in the satchel at her feet and removed a small battered Bible of her own. Turning to Job, she found one of her favourite passages. Job Chapter 39 verse 19. Hast thou given the horse his strength? Hast thou clothed his neck in thunder? She skipped over the bit about making the horse afraid as a grasshopper because who would want to do that? The glory of his nostrils is terrible. She skipped another line as her eyes closed and she jerked back to wakefulness. He paweth in the valley and rejoiceth in his strength he goeth on to meet the armed men. He mocketh at fear and is not affrighted.

Annie's fingers clenched on the thin onion paper pages. Was Evan afraid when he leaped out of the muddy trench into no man's land and a hail of bullets? And Steve, was Steve afraid when he died? In her heart she hoped was still alive, but her head insisted on disagreeing. Did he know he was going to die, or was it quick and fast and a surprise as he ran and fired. Dear Lord, please if it had to happen let it have been quick. Don't let him have lain broken and bleeding and alone as he passed. She blinked back tears at the memory of Sarah's brother who came home to Eganville just a month ago, missing both legs and blinded by the mustard gas. Just like Sammy's brother. He'd laid in the cold and wet for hours before anyone could get to him and transport him to a field hospital. She shivered and clasped her hand around the Bible. Dear Lord God Almighty, please keep Evan and George and Peter safe. Please let Steve come home to us.

"Ouch!" Annie came awake abruptly, a hand pressed to her aching forehead. The train must have come to a quick stop. When did I fall asleep? What time is it? Careful Mother wasn't paying attention she pushed back her sleeve and checked the time on George's mother's watch. Her fingers caressed the smooth mother of pearl warm from her body heat. Goodness, she must have slept for hours. The sun was slipping down the western sky ahead of them throwing long shadows across the bare ground by the railway tracks. She straightened up and glanced at Mother. The older woman's head nodded over the Bible still held open in her hands on her lap. Ivan was sprawled in his seat, legs spread wide, chin resting on his chest sleeping as only the young can sleep. Father had moved down the car and was talking to another gentleman who Annie didn't recognize. With another jerk the train began moving again, pulling away from a small station.

The next thing she was aware of was the train jolting to a halt and Father telling her to gather her things and be sure Ivan left nothing behind. She did as she was told and followed her family out into the chill Ontario night. May days could be hot but when the sun went to bed the nights were still chilly enough to make Annie pull her shawl tighter over her jacket.

"Where are we?" Her voice was still husky with sleep.

"Scotia," Father's reply was terse. "I have booked us rooms for the night. Hurry along now."

Annie followed behind her mother while keeping an eye on Ivan who was wont to stop and explore whatever might catch his attention regardless of what time of night it was. She was surprised when Father turned in at the gate of a two story clapboard house. What manner of hotel was this? The door was opened by a stout motherly looking woman who welcomed them warmly and ushered them into a tiny but neat dining room where sandwiches and tea awaited them. The meal was a blur of tiredness and Annie was happy to curl up on a pallet on the floor while Mother and Father lay down fully clothed on the single bed in the room. Before she dropped into sleep she heard Father whispering, apologizing to Mother for the spartan accommodations.

Morning dawned bright and clear and early. This close to mid-summer's day the light came early into the sky and lingered long into the evenings. A quick wash and equally quick morning repast found Annie once more clambering up the steps of a passenger car. This was a different train she realized. The name on the side was different, and the seats even more battered than the last one. In quick order the train got underway. Her eye caught the headline of the paper Father was reading. It was out of date by about three weeks but the headlines were full of the war in Europe and doom and gloom about the war going badly. She shoved down the cold fear in the pit of her belly. Yesterday there had been sentries posted at some of the big trestle bridges. She'd overheard Father and another man speaking of the fears the Germans would infiltrate the country and blow up the bridges. The idea seemed unlikely to her.

The engine blew its whistle long and loud. Peering out the window Annie gasped as three moose flashed past her window. The blackflies in the bush were fierce this time of year and the wild life routinely sought open places where the sun helped to keep the little pests at bay. She as very glad she was sitting in the relative comfort of the passenger car rather than out in the field digging the soil for the vegetable garden and getting eaten alive. She shuddered. Black flies and sand flies were a scourge. The little beggars could get through the tiniest of openings and before she'd been in the outdoors more than a few minutes they'd be feasting. Father would rub mineral oil or oil of citronella on the plow horses faces and in their ears and nostrils. Turning the earth seemed to drive the vicious things into a frenzy.

The distance from Scotia Junction and Bill Beatty's general store to Sprucedale was much shorter than their earlier journey from Golden Lake to Scotia Junction. The train puffed to halt at Sprucedale station in the early evening. Again Father had arranged for them to stay the night in a private home. A correspondent of his, a Mister Ford and his wife. Hetty and Clarence were waiting for them as they descended to the platform. Mother enfolded her eldest daughter in her arms and the pair went off toward the Ford's arm in arm leaving Annie to deal with Ivan and their hand luggage. She waited with the small huddle of bags, keeping Ivan on a short leash, while Father and Clarence dealt with the larger items being unloaded. Apparently the larger things would be stored at the station and then delivered to the new farm as soon as possible.

Annie took the opportunity to look around at her new home. Well, at least the closest thing to civilization that was near her new home, which was apparently out in the bush somewhere near someplace called Doe Lake.

Chapter Twelve

Summer 1917 passed in a blur of setting up house, getting used to the new barn and digging the large vegetable gardens needed to supply food over the winter. Ivan and Father built a root cellar and repaired the hen house and hog pen. The old barn was sturdy enough and suitable to house the horses, cattle and sheep which arrived soon after the Baldwins did.

The news from France and Belgium was grim. The Germans were winning and even in the backwoods of Ontario paranoia was rampant. Even a perceived sympathy for the Germans was enough to ostracize someone, or worse. There was a woman in the village whose son would never come home again, who was heard to mention she was sure the mothers of those poor German youngsters ground through the war machine were just as grief stricken as she was. It had been said in a moment of passion and the throes of grief, but no one would talk to her now for fear of being branded a spy or espionage agent. Annie felt sorry for her, but Hetty advised her to mind her own beeswax and keep her mouth shut. Of course, Mother agreed with her.

There had been no word from Evan for months and nothing new regarding Steve's missing in action status. The last letter from George said the fighting was fierce and they had suffered some heavy casualties. At least that's what she thought she gleaned from reading between the lines and around the censor's blacked out sections. There had been a brief note from Peter, forwarded from Eganville Post Office, which he sent from a convalescent home before going back to the front. It seemed that being a sapper meant going ahead to lay roads and track for the troops to advance. It also meant he was exposed to mustard gas again, which was what landed him in the convalescent home again. They were nice to him, he said, for which she was glad. Peter was a nice lad, more her own age than George.

* * *

Annie stood at the edge of the crowd on the main street of Sprucedale watching but not really participating in the Labour Day celebrations. Where did the summer go? She glanced down at her gloved hands, glad the covering hid the calluses and nicks she earned helping to get the garden in and then building and repairing the out buildings. The blister on the web of her right thumb was squishy courtesy of the shovel handle that needed sanding— again. With any luck it wouldn't break before she could get the gloves off, they were a pair of Mother's and Annie would catch the rough side of her tongue if they were spoilt. She sighed.

Mother had few fine things left from her early life in Ireland and she cherished them above all else. It was only family pride that prompted her to insist Annie wear them to cover her work roughened hands. No lady should be seen in public with hands like that, her mother declared.

"Let's go see if we can help the church ladies with the supper," her new friend Della whispered. "If I have to stand out here in the sun much longer I'll melt."

Annie nodded and poked Ivan in the ribs. He towered over her now, having experienced a growth spurt over the summer. Annie's head barely came to his shoulder now. "Hsst, Ivan. I'm going with Della to help with supper. Stay out of mischief."

"Don't I always?" He winked.

"On your head be it, then." She linked arms with her friend and slipped away while Father mounted the back of the buckboard that served as a stage for the occasion. Since they'd arrived in May, word of mouth had spread the news that Mister Baldwin was a doctor trained at Trinity College, Dublin, Ireland and also a preacher. Annie wasn't sure he was ordained, but having come from a family of Church of Ireland reverends, Father could preach hell fire and brimstone with the best of them. Mother often spoke of her father-in-law's country manor house in County Dromore.

Once the girls reached the long trestle tables set out beneath the shade of the spreading maples Annie was too busy to think of much else except what needed to be done next. By the time the festivities wound up, everything was in place for the hungry crowd to descend upon the tables and devour everything in sight. Annie and Della found a quiet place on the steps of the church out of the sun. The light breeze kept the mosquitos somewhat at bay, but the little devils still whined annoyingly in her ear. She slapped at a huge deer fly hovering over her bare arm where she'd rolled up her sleeves earlier. Annie had no wish to let the thing settle and bite, the result was a large welt and the actual bite hurt like the dickens, no wonder the poor horses snorted and stamped and threatened to bolt when the big flies swarmed around their bellies.

The pocket of her skirt crackled, reminding her of the precious still unread letter from George. The first one in what seemed like forever. Resisting the urge to open it right this moment, she listened with half-an ear to Della's chatter and picked at the food on her plate. By the time everyone was full and the babble of voices raised in conversation dissipated to a quiet murmur the sun was sending long orange-gold beams slanting across through the trees. Wriggling her aching feet in the confining boots, Annie let Della pull her upright. *If only I could take them off and go barefoot.* She shook out her full skirts and flipped the hem to remove some of the dust. *Mother would kill me dead if I went barefoot and embarrassed her by acting like a hoyden. But, my stars, these boots are* torture. The first step she took after picking her plate up from the church step decided her.

"Wait a moment, Della," she called and plunked back down on the step. In a matter of seconds the boots and her stockings were tucked under the edge of the steps. Annie wriggled her toes in the sandy soil in relief, made sure her long skirts hid her secret well enough, and picked up the discarded plate again. She joined Della who giggled and lifted her skirts to reveal long bare toes. Laughing like loons, the girls made their way toward the gaggle of church ladies. They pitched in helping with packing up the remaining bits of food and filling the big washing tub full of hot water heated on the fire nearby and soap. Another galvanized tub of clear water stood on the other end of the Beatty washstand for rinsing the dishes. Annie grinned. "Better to wash dishes than clothes," she whispered to Della.

The girls grabbed drying towels from the stack of flour sack dish towels and joined the line of women waiting for clean wet dishes. Once dry, they stacked them on the now cleared trestle tables for their owners to claim them later. Billy Munro's voice accompanied by his guitar and his brother on the squeeze box, or concertina as Mother insisted it be called, silenced the buzz of conversation. With the clean-up done, the women dispersed to find their men folks and enjoy some relaxation as well. The early fall dusk fell and with it a fresh breeze sprang up to cool the heat of the day.

Annie found a quiet place and folded her legs beneath her, leaning back against the cool smooth bark of a large white birch. Archie Eady brought out his fiddle and joined the Munro boys picking out a lively jig. Annie wondered if they were relatives of the Munroes near Eganville. Soon the open space was filled with dancers. Young couples sparking and oblivious to anyone else mingled with married couples. Even old Mister and Mrs. Allen were dancing the jig, their eighty year old feet remembering the quick deft steps from years of practice.

Annie closed her eyes and wished with all her heart George was with her, sitting beneath the tree with his fingers wound with hers. Her hand brushed the pocket with the hidden letter, she itched to pull it out but there was insufficient light to read the pale spidery writing. Later, she promised herself, when she was alone in her room with the light of the lamp. Then she could savour it without fear of interruption.

* * *

My Dear Annie,

I long to hear your voice. It seems like a dream to remember sitting with you in the woods and sharing my thoughts with you. I find it hard to believe this war will ever end. The hellfire and brimstone your father preaches about cannot be worse than what I am living through. I despair of it ever ending. But enough of this gloom and misery. I received your last letter and have read it over and over hearing your voice in my head and blocking out <the censor blacked out what George wrote next much to her vexation> I keep your notes in my breast pocket tied with a bit of twine. It comforts me to feel them safe when I close my eyes to sleep. When there is a chance to rest, one or more of us stay awake to keep watch for the enemy and beat off the rats and other vermin.

It's raining, again, so please ignore the blotches and ink smudges. One of the lads made a tiny container out of a spent bullet casing for me where I keep the lock of hair you sent last. It is safe on a thong around my neck and keeps you ever near my heart. Enclosed you will find a similar token. I caution you to clean it well before handling it as the cooties are most persistent. I will close now as the lad with the mail bag is waiting and I hear the Archies in the distance. Things will be <again the censors blacked out whatever he had written but Annie knew the Archies referred to German anti-aircraft fire.>.

May this find you as it leaves me

Pte. George Richardsont

Canadian Infantry (Eastern Ontario Regiment)

21st Btn

Her fingers trembled while searching for the bit of hair tucked into the thin paper. Finding a curly twist secured with a bit of twine, she got to her feet and moved closer to the lamp. Turning the strands this way and that, they appeared to be free of nits. To be sure, she found the small jar of coal oil she kept to refill her lamp and dipped the lock of sandy blonde hair until it was thoroughly soaked. Resealing the jar, she set it back and rummaged in her top drawer for an old handkerchief. She soaked up the excess oil before laying the precious curl on another clean bit of linen on the wide windowsill. Once it was dried Annie planned to sew a tiny pouch and wear it around her neck under her blouse like the amulets the Indians who came for doctoring wore.

Returning to the bed she tucked her feet under her and picked up George's letter again. Holding it near her face she inhaled the ingrained smell of the paper. Closing her eyes she imagined there was a faint underlying trace of his scent. Realistically, the odour of ink, mud and something sharp that made her eyes water over rode any subtle aroma, but it pleased Annie to think she could discern some trace of him. Opening her eyes her fingers lingered over a splotch on the paper that was darker and somehow more sinister than water marks. Blood? It could be? Please God, not his… "Quit being a silly goose." She shook her head and folded the paper again. "He'd tell you if he was hurt. Although, I wouldn't object to a blighty if it meant he could come home. Or maybe that's being selfish and unpatriotic. But oh, I wish the damn war would end and all the boys could come home."

Annie tucked George's letter under her pillow. It had taken some doing, but finally her parents had been persuaded that writing to the boys on the front was only the Christian thing to do. There had been a great deal of excitement when the first of George's letters arrived and it had taken all her wit to keep Father from throwing it into the fire. So now, Annie wrote to Peter, George, the Foley boys and the other local boys spending their youth in the muddy fields of France and Belgium.

Settling down to sleep Annie reflected on the young men present at the Labour Day celebrations. It was hard not to feel resentful that they had escaped the conscription using the excuse they were needed on the farms. Everywhere women were stepping up and filling the empty shoes of their men, some who had made the supreme sacrifice, copped a packet as the lads were wont to say. Even Rotha was off somewhere secret near Trenton where she was involved in Lord only knew what. The woman was closed mouth as a clam about her war duties. Personally, Annie thought most of the men not doing their part were cowards. She sighed. I suppose I can't blame the Dean boy, with his weak chest he'd never last a minute in the wet and the cold. But the rest of them...? She'd like to give them a piece of her mind.

Chapter Thirteen

"Annabelle, haven't you finished with the fruit cake yet?" Mother bustled into the kitchen patting a stray hair back into place.

"Almost, Mother." She placed the last thin slice on the fine china plate.

"Hurry along, then. Bring it in directly and a tea tray too, if you please." Mother scooped the platter of shortbread and sugar cookies off the counter and disappeared back toward the parlour.

Annie sighed and leaned on the counter for a moment gazing unseeing out the window over the sink. Snow fell in gentle swirling flakes adding to the drifts already accumulated. The neatly shovelled paths to the outbuildings and the privy were rapidly filling in. One more chore she'd chivvy Ivan into helping her with. How could it be Christmas already? The fourth Christmas of the war. Two Christmases without her big brothers. After the first devastating telegram there had been no word of Steve. Annie feared the worst but refused to acknowledge what common sense told her must be the truth. And Evan, fun loving handsome Evan. His last letter to Father came in August and no word since. A chill hand seized her heart. Anything could have happened to him, but she clung to the old adage 'no news is good news'. Better no news at all than the finality of another telegram bearing the ill-fated news. She spared a thought for Della, her sweetheart Aaron Foley was reported killed in action just last month. Poor old heart-broken Mister Foley went to Della hat in hand bearing the terrible information.

Annie swiped the back of her hand across wet cheeks. Enough of this. It does nobody any good to go borrowing trouble.

"Annabelle!"

"Coming, Mother." She wiped her eyes on the hem of her apron and pressed a hand over the tiny calico pouch holding George's hair. Picking up the plate of fruitcake she wedged it on the tea tray and made sure the teapot was hot. Lifting the heavy tray she pasted a smile on her face and moved toward the parlour where Father's guests were assembled. She backed into the parlour and set the tea down on the sideboard next to Mother's prized crystal candelabra. Careful not to brush the delicate thing, Annie poured and circulated cups and saucers of fragrant strong black Irish tea, the leaves from Mother's dwindling cache being carefully measured out. She followed up with milk and sugar and a small plate of lemon wedges. Mother sniffed in disapproval at the extravagance, but Father had somehow managed to find two small somewhat shrivelled lemons. A minor miracle in the midst of winter and the shortages caused by the war. Annie breathed a sigh of relief at Mother's discrete wave of dismissal.

She shook out her skirts and gathered them in her hands prior to ascending the stairs. Rotha was coming home tomorrow and Annie needed to set up the extra cot in her room. It would be a little like old times sharing a room with her sister. There was a letter from Alice Father planned to read aloud to them later. Of course Hetty and the stiff necked Clarence would come for Christmas Eve service tomorrow and then arrive at the house the next day to exchange gifts and stay for Christmas dinner. She spared a thought for the poor Tom turkey who was even now happily poking around in the barn oblivious to his fate. At least his demise would be quick unlike the lot of those PBI — the Poor Blood Infantry — who lay in the no man's land between the opposing armies slowly dying of their wounds. Della's sister was an ambulance driver in France and sent back accounts of what was really happening on the Western Front. Annie shuddered. It certainly wasn't the glory and honour of fighting for King and country the newspapers would have people believe. She kept these thoughts to herself as it only upset Mother and Father insisted it was all balderdash and the Germans would soon be on the run.

Annie opened the linen press in the hallway and retrieved clean sheets, a pillow and case and a warm blanket. Ivan had set up the narrow cot against the far wall of her room earlier. It was only the work of a few minutes for her to make the bed up and fluff the pillow. The sun set early this late in December and the encroaching darkness matched her mood. Crossing to the window she paused a moment to stare at the blue shadows bruising the pearly snow drifts.

Poor Rotha must be freezing on the drafty train right now. By this time tomorrow though she'd be home and snug as a bug. Annie pulled one side of the heavy curtain across and reached to secure the other to stave off the fingers of wind that found their way through every nook and cranny. Movement by the farm gate stayed her hand. She leaned closer to the single pane glass and rubbed at the frost accumulated on the inside. What is that? She squinted. A moose? No, a bear? Whatever it was that moved in the gathering dusk seemed to stumble along on two legs. It must be a person, but Rotha couldn't possibly be in Sprucedale yet, let along come this far, and Father wasn't expecting anyone else that she knew of. The figure stumbled in the deep drifts between the ruts of the lane and almost landed headfirst into the snow. Snugging the curtain closed Annie hurried downstairs.

She slipped into the parlour and whispered in her Mother's ear. "There's someone coming up the lane. Are we expecting any one?"

"Hsst. Go and see who it is and what they want. No doubt someone coming for a potion or some doctoring. If it's not life threatening take them into the kitchen and let them wait on Mister Baldwin's pleasure. Go now, girl. Be quick about it." Her mother gave her an imperative shove before picking up her tea cup again.

"Fine," Annie huffed under her breath. She snatched a woollen shawl from the newel post and wrapped it around her. The air in the hall was frigid her breath puffed out before her as she breathed. Just like Saint George and his dragon, she giggled at the thought. The dusk was heavy now when she peered out the small window by the door. Most people come for doctoring went to the back door, but the muffled figure continued its unsteady way toward the main door where she waited. That was curious, it wasn't one of the natives then, they always came to the back and usually had a brace of rabbits or quail in hand. Maybe it's one of the Finlanders from Gordon Dean's cottages down on the lake. If so, she'd best go fetch the Finnish-English dictionary. The Finlanders came to work the logging camps and escape the economic hardships of their home country. There was only a handful of them, but Father seemed to think there would be an influx of them in the next few years. Between their broken English and Father's broken Finnish they seemed to manage to communicate. Annie took a last quick look out the frosty window before going to fetch the small book. She stopped and whirled back, hand pressed to her breast as she fought for breath.

Dear Lord, it looks like an army issue haversack — what did George call it — a kit bag. Her heart skipped a beat hoping it was George before common sense told her this man was far too tall to be George Richardson. Even bent over as he was under the burden on his back. Annie fumbled with the matches and had to try twice to light the wick of the lamp, her fingers shaking with more than the cold. Holding the lamp high she cracked the door open and peered out. The figure at the edge of the wide snow covered porch lifted his head and stared at her with haunted eyes.

"Annie? Is it really you? I'm not dreaming?" The man fell to his knees letting his gear scatter around him.

"Evan? Dear God, Evan!" She pulled the door wide open ignoring the cold wind that swept down the hall and hurried to his side. "Oh, Evan. I'm so glad to see you. I can't believe you're home. Here, let me help you up, get you inside and warm you up." Setting the still lit lamp on the bench by the door she oxtercogged her brother upright, swaying under the strain of taking all of his weight. "Father, Mother! Come quick! Help!" Without waiting for a response Annie managed to get him moving and through the door. He eased himself down on a the hall entry bench, leaning his head back and closing his eyes as if the effort to keep them open was too much for him. "Mother!" Annie scurried back out and gathered Evan's kit out of the snow and rescued the spluttering lamp from the snowy bench by the door. Heaving the kit bag and other paraphernalia inside she pulled the door shut, kneeling by Evan's feet and pulling off the snow encrusted hobnailed trench boots. "Father!" She called as loudly as she could, afraid to leave her brother long enough to open the parlour door.

"Annie, whatever are you carrying on about?" Ivan poked his head into the hall. "Father says to quit caterwauling and..." He stopped in mid-sentence, mouth falling open in shock. "Evan?" he whispered before charging back into the parlour screeching at the top of his lungs.

"Annabelle, what have you done to set your brother off like that?" Mother stepped out of the doorway. "What's this? Whatever is going on here?" The older woman ventured a few steps closer clutching her fine woollen shawl to her throat. "Annabelle..."

"It's Evan, Mother. It's Evan, and he's frozen half to death. Get Father, he's too heavy for me to get into the kitchen near the big stove." Her last words were spoken to the empty hall as Ella Baldwin fled back into the parlour. "There now, my lad. We'll have you warm in no time and food in your belly. They'll be here to help in a moment, just you wait and see." She frowned at the exhausted expression on his handsome face and his curiously blank look. At least it used to be handsome, now it was gaunt with dark shadows like bruises under his eyes and cheekbones sharp enough she wouldn't be surprised if they broke through the ashen skin stretched tautly across them. Discarding the icy boots, Annie peeled off the thick socks and wrapped his feet in her shawl.

"Evan, lad. Is it you?" Father burst into the hall way followed by two of his male guests. Mother hovered behind them, dabbing at her eyes daintily with an Irish lace handkerchief.

"Aye, what's left of me." Evan's voice was thin and rusty as if he hadn't used it in some time. "Christ, I'm knackered." His chin dropped unto his chest.

"He's half-frozen, Father. We need to get him into the kitchen by the stove and something hot into him." Annie moved out of the way to allow the men folks to get her brother on his feet. She squeezed Ivan's shoulder. The boy looked gobsmacked, his face pale in the flickering light.

"Is he alright, then, Annie? He looks real sick." Her younger brother's voice trembled.

"He's exhausted, Ivan. And frozen half to death. Nothing some heat and a good feed can't cure," she assured him with false bravado. Privately, Annie feared there was far more amiss with her older brother than cold and hunger. Shell shock, that's what Della's sister wrote home about. Brave young men with night terrors and gibbering like idiots, screaming and staring at something only they could see.

"Go see how Mother is faring," she ordered Ivan. Her mother had disappeared into the parlour and one of the lady guests was waving smelling salts under her nose when Annie glanced in the door on the way by. "It will do her heart good to have one son hale and hearty beside her. Don't worry, I'll see to Evan. It will be fine. You'll see." Annie gave him a gentle shove. "Go sit by her feet and entertain her and her guests with one of your witty stories. You know how she loves that."

Annie glanced at the mess in the hall and decided it could wait. Evan's wellbeing was far more important at the moment. Heaven only knew when Mother would recover from her fainting spell brought on by the shock. You'd think she'd be overjoyed to have Evan alive and safe at home. She shrugged, if she lived to be a hundred Annie would never fathom how Mother's mind worked. She pushed open the kitchen door and stepped into the welcome warmth.

"Ella, you should wait…Oh, it's you Annabelle. Come lend a hand here." Father glanced up and then motioned her to his side. "If you gentlemen would like to rejoin the ladies?" He raised his eyebrows at his guests.

"If you're sure you no longer have need of us," Clifford Hanlon said, putting some distance between himself and the noisome bundle that was her brother.

The heat in the kitchen melted the snow and ice clinging to Evan's clothes and released some of the more noxious odors emanating from him. Annie moved aside to let the men pass.

"Get some blankets and as many bed warmers as you can lay hands on. I'll get him out of these clothes." Father unbuttoned the army issue top coat, unwinding the long scarf from around Evan's neck at the same time.

Annie hurried to fetch as many thick wool blankets as she could carry. Dumping them on the large harvest table she went off in search of copper bed warmers and the pottery pigs that would be filled with hot water. Evan's breath whistled in his chest and his body shook with chills. By the time she filled the copper pans with coals from the stove, Father was wrestling the stiff khaki off one shoulder. Evan's left hand closed like a vise over his father's and Annie started in surprise.

"Don't." The command was harsh. "I can't look at it." Evan's head wavered on his neck and he closed his eyes, face twisted in a grotesque grimace.

"What is it, son. What can't you look at?" Father met Annie's worried gaze over his head, then glanced at the other sleeve of the coat.

Annie clamped her lips shut against the hiss of denial that rose in her throat. Her stomach hurt like it had when one of the milk cows swung her head into it. The right sleeve of Evan's coat lay flat and empty. How had she not noticed that fact before? Oh Evan! Annie's heart broke into a million tiny pieces. The anguish was followed quickly by anger. What kind of God let horrid things like this happen? Sent young men hardly more than boys out to be mowed down by machine gun fire and cut dead by whiz bang shells? She dropped to her knees by his side.

"Evan, Evan. It doesn't matter. You're home and you're alive. That's all that matters." She pressed a palm to his cold cheek.

"It matters to me, Annie." He leaned into her hand while a tear glistened on his dark eyelashes. "It matters to me."

"Here now, son. Let me take a look. The army doctors saw to it, I suppose? Perhaps something can be done to repair some of the damage." Father eased the coat and jacket off Evan's body.

"There's nothing to repair, Father. It's gone. From above the elbow down. Gone."

The stark finality in his tone sent chills over Annie. A goose walking on my grave, that's what it feels like. "I don't care, Evan. Two arms or no arms, you're home safe, that's enough for me. The rest of it, well, we'll manage. I promise," she said fiercely. She made herself watch while Father removed Evan's shirt and revealed the livid red stump. It looked inflamed to her, but she looked to her father for his opinion. From the grim line of his mouth, he wasn't happy with the condition of the flesh either.

He wrapped two blankets around Evan and set to work on removing the trousers. "Annabelle, perhaps you can busy yourself filling the pigs. No need to embarrass your brother or yourself. I can handle this part of it."

"Of course." She scrambled to her feet and set about unscrewing the caps of the thick pottery flat bottom crocks. After rinsing them

171

once with hot water to warm the cold pottery she filled them and re-capped them. Wrapping them in towels she placed one under Evan's feet and one on each side of them. Father had him swaddled in blankets and sent Ivan with the copper bed warmers to heat the sheets on the makeshift bed on the horsehair sofa in Father's study. Annie shook her head, when did Ivan leave the parlour come into the kitchen? Well, no matter. At least the bed would be ready when Evan was able to move that far.

"Stay with him, I'm going to fetch my medical bag." Father let his hand rest on her shoulder. It was the closest thing to thanks and appreciation she could expect from him.

With one eye on her brother, Annie made a large mug of strong sweet tea pressing the offering into his hand, closing his fingers over it.

"What shall I do with your uniform, Evan? I can wash it in the morning…"

"Burn it. I never want to see the damned thing again." He ground the words out between clenched teeth.

"If you wish." Annie bundled the wet filthy items into a ball and deposited them in a corner of the back mud room. Father could decide if burning them was the right thing to do. It was more of a decision than Annie wished to make at the moment.

"Evan, dear. Are you quite alright? You gave me quite a turn showing up unannounced like that." Mother hovered in the doorway. "The company has left," she spoke to her husband as he returned with the medical bag. "Under the circumstances it seemed the best thing to do."

Father nodded and set the bag on the table, opening it to display the rows of tiny bottles and other equipment. Mother moved further into the kitchen and placed a tentative hand on Evan's shoulder.

"It's nice to have you home for Christmas, son. However did you manage to get leave?" A smile trembled on her lips.

"Not leave, Mother. I've got a blighty."

"A what?" Mother's eyes widened and then she blinked twice.

"A blighty, Mother. I'm invalided out." A harsh laugh escaped him. "Got it hopping over the bags, left a piece of me for the Huns to chew on."

"Evan, speak English please. Hopping over bags, my stars. And what piece...Oh my!"

Evan flipped back the blanket with his good hand to reveal the angry stump of his right arm. "Hopping over the bags means going over the top, scrambling out of the dubious safety of the trench into enemy fire. And...well, you can see what piece of me I left behind."

"Oh dear." Mother sat down heavily in a kitchen chair as if her legs wouldn't hold her. "Oh, dear."

"Mother, if you're feeling faint why don't you have Ivan bring you a cup of strong tea and your smelling salts." Annie spared her a glance before tucking the blanket back around him.

173

"I believe I will have some tea. Harold, what is that dreadful odour?" Mother waved a hand delicately in front of her nose. "I really am glad you're home, Evan."

"I have trench foot," Evan muttered. "I can't hardly stand the stink of myself." His face twisted with self-loathing.

"We'll deal with it. Now, let me see that arm, if you would," Father took hold of his son's arm above the raw stump.

Evan leaned his head back and closed his eyes. Annie watched closely as Father palpated the swollen flesh and pressed on the half-healed scars of his arm. Evan's breath hissed through his teeth though he never moved.

Mother's skirts rustled as she departed in a rush, Ivan back from his bed warmer mission followed with her tea.

"It'll do. For now." Harold Baldwin declared of the wound and smeared some bear grease mixed with some sort of pungent herbs. He took some of the mouldy bread he kept in the larder and wrapped the stump in clean lint bandages. "Now, the feet."

Annie bit her lip at the sight of the white swollen lumps below Evan's ankles. How in the name of God did he manage to walk on those? Some of the skin was going dark which she knew wasn't a good sign at all. Father dried them carefully and prodded gently at the darkened skin.

"Not as bad as it could be, son. They'll need some debridement, but we can certainly save them for you. Now let's get you into bed, shall we?"

"I could sleep in this chair," Evan's words slurred. "It's been forever since I actually slept. Not safe…"

Father nodded to Annie. She moved to Evan's side and together they got him to his feet. Ivan showed up and helped steady the invalid as they made their slow painful way down the hall to the study. Annie stood back while Father and Ivan got Evan settled and covered warmly. The fire was burning well, Ivan moved to bank it a bit so it would last through the night. Father fed a few nuggets of precious coal into the heart of the flames.

"I'll just go clean up the kitchen and tidy the front hall," Annie excused herself from the room.

An hour later she peeked in the study door. Evan lay still as the dead under the mound of blankets. At first she thought him asleep but when the fire flared in response to the wind whipping down the chimney she caught the glint of his eye. Ivan lay curled in the big Morris chair head cushioned on his arm, fast asleep. Deciding not to disturb her brothers, Annie withdrew and went up the stairs. She'd heard Father's tread on the stairs earlier and was surprised to detect the murmur of voices from behind her parent's closed door. Whatever are they talking about? Evan, I suspect and how to deal with his new reality. She hesitated — it was wrong to eavesdrop, but…it would be

175

advantageous to know what Mother thought of the situation in order to decide how to buffer Evan from her if need be. Her darling boy was no longer perfect and Annie was uncertain how her maternal parent would react to that once it really set in. You'd think she'd be over the moon that one of her boys has come home. Annie shook her head. The voices faded and the thin sliver of lamplight under the door darkened.

She continued to her room, glancing at the extra bed. Thank goodness Rotha would be arriving in the morning and could take some of the burden of caring for Evan and dealing with Mother. She sighed. Now Hetty, that was another kettle of fish altogether. Father would probably ride into the village first light to take her the news so she wouldn't be blindsided when she arrived for Christmas Day. It was anyone's guess how her oldest sister might respond. Oh, she'd be overjoyed at the news Evan was home, but Hetty had the same opinion as her mother regarding less than perfect things, material or human.

After stirring up the fire and then smooring it to keep til morning, Annie dropped into bed. She swore she'd only just closed her eyes when the most Godawful caterwauling had her bolting upright, quilt clutched to her throat.

Evan! It must be Evan. No, that's Ivan screaming. What in the world…?

She was up and bundling into a warm robe in two shakes of a lamb's tail. Wrenching open her door she fled down the stairs toward the

176

study. Annie burst into the dimly lit room to find Ivan peering out from behind the wing chair where he crouched, hair on end and his eyes wide with terror. She waved at him to stay where he was and turned her attention to Evan.

Her brother's eyes were bulging in his thin face, mouth twisted in a rictus as he screamed in that high thin wail that sent shivers coursing over her skin. One hand clawed at the air as if he were trying to grasp something while the stump on the other side flailed to be free of the confining quilts. Dear Lord in Heaven. Is this what Della's sister was talking about?

"Evan! Evan, it's me, Annie." She stepped closer. "Evan." The muscles under the hand she laid on his bad arm were hard as ice in the dead of winter and he didn't seem to see or hear her. "Hush, now. It's me. You're safe, Evan. You're safe." As she spoke she ran a hand over his hair. "Hush now. Hush."

Her ministrations did nothing to lessen the screaming. His face took on a blueish tinge while the breathing became more erratic. The chords in his neck stood out in sharp relief as he struggled to breathe. Where is Father? "Ivan, go fetch Father. Now!" She spared him a glance.

"No need. I'm here now. Annabelle, step aside please. Let me handle this."

Annie was relieved to give up her place at her brother's side. She stood back twisting her fingers in the ties of her robe. Ivan flung both arms around her waist and pressed against her. His trembling shaking her as well.

"Evan, wake up now. That's a good lad," Father shook Evan's shoulders.

Annie tightened her arm around Ivan's shoulders. Father might as well be talking to himself. Dear God, poor Evan. Father glanced over at them, his gaze resting on Ivan the longest.

"Ivan, why don't you go up and sit with your mother, if you would. She's quite undone by all this and I'd rather not leave her alone."

"It's alright, you go ahead. Evan will be fine, he's just having a nightmare. Father will calm him down. Go on, Mother will have need of you," Annie urged her brother.

Ivan nodded and after one last desperate look at the figure on the sofa fled the room.

"Go fetch a basin of cold water and some clothes." Father strained to keep Evan from falling off the sofa with his writhing, dodging the wildly swung fist of his son's good arm.

She returned in a few minutes, water sloshing over the rim of the bowl she carried. Kneeling by her father, she set the water on the floor and wet the thick squares of towelling. At Father's nod she placed a folded cloth on Evan's forehead and wiped his face with another. Father kept up a string of inconsequential platitudes delivered in a soothing tone. Outside wolves howled close to the house in response to the cries of distress emanating from within.

Father squared his shoulders as if reaching some kind of inner decision. "Stand clear, Annabelle."

Startled, she did as she was told, getting to her feet and moving a few paces away, gaze fixed on the two struggling features. The lamp guttered and almost went out, throwing the room into more shadow. She attended to the lamp and poked up the fire. The sharp crack of a slap sent her whirling about, poker brandished before her. Horrified, she couldn't make her feet move as Father slapped Evan again.

"Father!" she managed to get the strangled word out. Horror turned to relief as sense came back into her brother's eyes. His gaze landed on her and he surged up off the sofa carrying Father with him half-way across the room.

"Bloody Boche! Bastard Germans! I'll kill you with my bare hands, Fritz. Let me go!" He hissed at his father like a snake. "Let me go. Can't you see what they've done? Look out there." Evan gestured wildly at something only he could see. "Can't you hear them screaming for help? For God's sake let me go. I've got to get to him." With a superhuman effort he wrenched free of Father and hurled himself at the sofa, clambering over the back of it, limbs windmilling in his agitation. "I'm coming Billy. I'm coming, hang on." He slid over the back of the sofa, landing in a heap on the floor. "I'm coming, Billy. Keep yelling."

Father pulled the sofa further from the wall and jumped back when Evan swung at him with a vicious left-handed punch. "Fecking Boche. You can't have him. Billy! No, no, oh no…"

Evan's fierce anger fled leaving him a boneless wreck sobbing inconsolably.

"Stay with him, Annabelle. I need to fetch something." Father whirled and was gone before she could reply.

On tentative feet she approached Evan who lay where he fell, wedged between the wall and the sofa. He was cold under her hand when she touched him. Sinking down Annie gathered him in her arms and rocked him as she used to rock Ivan when he was young.

"There now, there now. It'll all come right. Just you wait and see if I'm not right. You're safe, you're home now. Everything will be right as rain come the morning," she lied without a qualm. Who was Billy and what in God's name happened over there? Going by Evan's reactions, Annie was fairly sure she knew Billy's fate. He must have been a mate of Evan's. How horrible to not be able to go to the aid of a friend. She stroked her brother's face, his harsh sobs reduced to silent tears now. Thank God! Father entered carrying another lamp and a shiny hypodermic needle in hand. She wriggled around to give him access to Evan's good arm, disengaging it from where it clutched her.

It was only work of a few seconds for him to find the vein and slide the needle home. Evan became a heavier weight on her and his breathing evened out and slowed. Father offered her a hand up which she gratefully accepted.

Leaning down she pulled the quilts and blankets free of him.

"We need to get him off the floor," Father said. He moved the piece of furniture further away from the sprawled body. Grasping Evan under the arms, he flipped him over and dragged him away from the wall a good distance. "I'll need your help to get him on the sofa, girl."

Annie nodded and took hold of her brother's good arm. Between them they oxtercogged him upright and onto the sofa. Releasing a sigh of relief, Annie retrieved the pillow and tucked it behind his head. Father gathered the quilts and helped her tuck them around him. They stood side by side looking down at the injured man.

"Someone has to stay with him," Father remarked without looking at her.

"It can't be Ivan. The poor boy has already had more than he can be expected to handle." Annie straightened her shoulders and rubbed at a sore spot on her hip. "I'll sit with him until morning. Then someone else will have to take over."

"Rotha will be here on the morning train." A frown crossed Harold Baldwin's brow. "Someone will have to take the sleigh into the village to meet her."

"Let Ivan do it. It'll take his mind off things and you know how he dotes on Rotha and loves to drive the sleigh," Annie suggested.

Father nodded at her and she found herself under the scrutiny of his assessing gaze. "You did well tonight, Annabelle. I thank you for your assistance."

"Harold?" Mother's voice echoed down the staircase and through the open study door.

He cast his eyes upward and moved toward the door. "I best go explain what happened to your mother."

Chapter Fourteen

It was the first of many nights Annie was to sit with her brother and help him through the night terrors. Shell Shock, Della confirmed when Annie met her in the village to collect the mail one bright sunny January morning. Her sister was home from France for some secret reason Della wouldn't, or couldn't, share. It seemed a good idea for Frances to come and sit with Evan for part of the day. Annie observed them curiously. It was like they belonged to some secret club that anyone who hadn't been overseas could be part of. In a way she envied them that comfort.

Would it be like that when George came home? A part of him he couldn't share with her, a distance she would be at sixes and sevens over how to bridge. The thought disturbed Annie more than she cared to admit. Just let him come home. Soon. And Peter, and Steve. Why haven't we heard anything about Steve? Surely if he were dead they'd have figured that out by now.

* * *

Annie straightened and propped a forearm on the top of the handle of the hoe. The June sun burned bright in the brilliant blue of the sky that contrasted so sharply with the dark spruce and pine surrounding small patch of cleared fields. She wiped the trickle of sweat from her cheek with the corner of her apron and bent back to the task of ridding the beans from weeds.

The back breaking but mindless work provided time to sort through her thoughts. She bent to pry a rock out of the turned earth and pitched into the basket two rows over already half full of stones.

There were visitors last night, and not the usual kind. Annie sighed. There was always a steady stream of people coming up the long lane from the lake. Finlanders from Dean's cottages on Doe Lake; logging was hard and dangerous work, natives occasionally, and other preachers, all coming to confer with Father. She disliked the preachers the most, they always set Father off on a tirade of fire and brimstone and eternal damnation.

She snorted and dug the blade of hoe into the earth with more force than was necessary. With the sun beating down on her back, the biting flies rising from the turned soil and the humidity sticking the clothes to her body Annie figured she was already in Hell. She stopped short at the blasphemy of that thought and glanced around, guilt swirling in her gut. Surely Father couldn't read her mind? Although, there was no telling with him, he seemed to know more than was humanly possible about what went on around the homestead and in the small village of Sprucedale that lay nearby.

Her gaze rested on Evan carefully sowing rows of carrots and beets in the already turned part of the garden. Once the benighted stones were out of this part of the garden there were hills of potatoes and squash to plant. Bushel baskets of seed onions and coarse burlap bags of seed potatoes waited in the shade of the large maple by the gate. Bending back to her task, she chopped at the sandy soil and turned up yet another batch of rocks.

"Annie!" She straightened at the sound of her name and squinted against the glare of the sun.

"Della! How nice!" She swiped the back of her hand across her hot face and gathered her dusty skirts in one hand stepping over the turned earth.

Evan joined her, pushing the sling holding the seeds around to his back. Annie hid a smile at the realization Frances was with Della. She snuck a look at Evan out of the corner of her eye, relieved to see Frances' happiness reflected in his expression. He reached out his left arm to help Annie step over the low fence supporting the trellis for the red runner beans. For once his shirt sleeves were rolled up, even the one he usually wore pinned closed over the stump. His skin was a healthy brown from the hours spent in the sun and there was a tattoo on his forearm she'd never noticed before.

"What brings you here?" Annie plunked down in the grass under a maple.

"Father has some business with Mister Baldwin, so we thought we'd hitch a ride," Della replied settling beside her. "My stars, it's a scorcher today. Listen to the heat bugs sing."

"Come join us, Frances. Would you like a cup of water?" Evan held out the tin cup he lifted dripping from the oak bucket.

"What's that on your arm?" Frances sounded faint, her face pale in the dappled shade.

"My arm?" Evan looked down stupidly. "What's wrong with my arm?"

Annie thought it was an improvement her brother didn't assume the woman was asking about his missing limb. Evan dropped the cup into the bucket and reached out to steady Frances who backed up a step out of range. "What's the mark on your forearm?"

"Oh, that." A smile crossed his face. "Steve and I got them in London before we shipped out. A lot of the lads got them, some shop near Waterloo, man by the name of George Burchett. Why?"

"Did you and your brother get the exact same image?"

Della scrambled to her feet to support her sister. "What is it, Frances? What's wrong?"

Frances ignored her and kept her gaze fixed on Evan.

"Yeah, we did. A maple leaf and the words For King and Country. Brothers forever and our initials."

"Oh dear." Frances' eyes filled with tears. "Oh dear me."

Annie leaped up and gripped her arm. "Have you seen one like it? Did you see Steve in hospital in France?" Her heart thundered in anticipation. Steve was alive somewhere, she knew it. Frances saw him, maybe spoke to him. She must know where he was.

"Where did you see this tattoo?" Evan moved closer to Frances.

"I need to sit." Frances plopped down on the rough bench beneath the tree. "Give me a minute and I'll tell you."

"You saw Steve. He's alive, oh I can't wait to tell Mother and Father. And Ivan." Annie fairly danced in place.

Tears filled Frances' eyes and she looked imploringly up at Evan. Something passed between them Annie couldn't fathom. Evan sank down on the bench beside her and placed a hand on Frances' arm.

"Tell us what you know, please," he said gently.

She nodded and swallowed hard. "It was in France, the Somme." She paused and closed her eyes. Annie noted her brother squeezed the woman's hand. "We set up a CCS near the attack on High Wood."

"What's a CCS?" Annie interrupted.

"What, oh?" Frances blinked and refocused her attention as if returning from some place far removed from the sunny June garden in the Ontario bush. "Casualty Clearing Station. They bring the men in by stretcher or ambulance, if the roads are passable. Sometimes the lads would show up carrying their mates over their shoulders." She shuddered.

Evan got up abruptly and stalked to the edge of the garden, back to the girls. "Go on," he said, voice flat and emotionless.

"One PBI I'll never forget, Lord I can't get that boy out of my mind." She scrubbed her hands over her face. "Tall fellow, came staggering in with his mate over his shoulders. Walked right up to me as if he knew me or had been looking for me and set his burden down at my feet. 'Fix him,' he said. 'I know you can help him. He's a wife at home expecting a baby. Fix him.' The poor thing didn't look old enough to be married, let alone a daddy. He was barely more than a child himself. I tended to him, but there was nothing I could do. Nothing any of us could do. A whiz bang, that's a shell used by the German seventy-seven millimetre guns that moved so fast the PBI had no time to even duck, it took both his legs. The poor bugger bled out under my hands. I didn't realize the soldier who brought him in was wounded at first. He just stood there swaying and insisting I fix his mate. When I tried to get him to come in out of the rain, he was plastered with mud from head to toe, that was part of the reason I didn't see the blood at first, he just crumpled up at my feet. We got him inside and stripped off his wet things." She stopped and gulped, pressing a hand to her stomach. "He had a gut wound, his

188

intestines were poking out. How he ever managed to walk so far carrying his gear and his mate…well…I don't know…it shouldn't have been possible. Somewhere, he'd lost his ID tags, maybe when the shells hit. I don't know. After he collapsed he didn't speak at all, except to mumble a name when I asked. It sounded like Steve, but I had no way of knowing if it was his name or the poor boy he carried in. I sat with him until…until it was over. He had a tattoo just like that on his left arm."

"What did he look like," Annie whispered, holding Della's hand so hard her fingers hurt.

"Tall, like I said. Blue-grey eyes, blond hair. He had a scar running down his right thigh…"

Annie's heart shattered like thin ice on a fall morning. Though her heart refused to accept the fact the unknown soldier was Steve, her head knew it was so. Sobs shook her and twisted her guts. "Oh Steve," she whispered.

"What happened to the body?" Evan's voice held a sharp edge. He strode back into the shade and sat on the bench.

"I believe he was taken to Heily Station and buried there. We had to move the CCS quickly and I…I…I'm sorry, I lost track of him in the chaos. I remember the Nursing Sister in charge saying the severely wounded were evacuated to Heily Station. She told me she sent 'my PBI' with that lot, just in case." Frances held up a hand to stop Annie's outburst. "He's gone. I was with him when he took his last breath. I'm sure.

189

Now I see it, he looked like you Evan, only a bit rougher."

"That would be Steve." A pained smile crossed his face. He straightened his shoulders. "I'll go inform Father. It is a comfort to know at last what happened to my brother."

Frances stood and put her hand on his good arm, tipping her head back to look into his face. "He died a hero, Evan. If that's any comfort to you. He was a very brave man."

"It will most likely be of some comfort to Mother, she sets a great store by such things. Me, I'd rather he was a coward and had come home to us." His mouth twisted bitterly.

Annie listened to the exchange as if from a great distance. Nothing seemed real, not the bright sun in the brilliant blue sky or the breeze shaking the green leaves overhead. Her thoughts cast in restless circles much like a hound searching for a scent. Frances' words painted vivid pictures in her mind. Images the sepia newspaper photographs failed to evoke. The hell on earth George and the others were living in was suddenly all too real. Annie fought to keep from spilling her stomach into the springy grass.

"I'm so sorry." Frances enveloped her in a hug, stroking her hair. "I'm so sorry I couldn't help him."

Annie wanted to scream and rage. Why Steve, others made it out. Other men got wounded and survived. God was unfair. Steve was a good man, a good brother, a good son. What sense did it make to take someone like him when there were all those cowards hiding safe at home. Annie clenched her fists and beat on her thighs. Della put her arms around her from the other side and the three women rocked in shared grief in the shade of the old maple.

* * *

Annie pressed the precious letter to her breast. George's bold letters scrawled across the front brought him somehow closer to her. He's alive. He's alive. Surely the war will be over soon. It's been going on so long now. The summer of 1918 was drawing to a close. The loft was full of hay, the fields of wheat and oats waved ripening heads of gold in the August sun. The fifth August of the war to end all wars as the papers were calling the bloody conflict. She leaned against the back of the wood shed, stealing a few private moments to read George's letter and dream of him coming home to her.

My Dear Annie,
Hoping this finds you as it leaves me. Thank you for your last parcel. The socks are very welcome. I don't think my feet will ever be dry again. I was sorry to hear the news about Steve, so many good men have lost their lives in the conflict it hardly bears thinking about. Please give my condolences to your parents, and of course to Evan and Ivan and your sisters. It eases my heart to know one of your brothers made it back home. Even without an arm, he is

well out of this mess. The fighting has been bloody and fierce and the damnable rain just won't quit. Mud in my face, mud in my shoes, I swear there's mud in my tea. I had news of Pete, the poor sod was gassed again at <censor blacked out> he was at <blacked out> Convalescent House in <censor blacked out> but is now back going about his duties. He tells me he was awarded a Good Conduct Badge, though I'm not sure for what. I can't remember if I told you that already. He promises to write to you himself, but you know how Pete hates to put pen to paper.

I miss you very much and hope God sees his way to let us be together in the near future. Our company is on the move again, heading to the <censor blacked out but Annie thought she could make out the word Somme — the censor must have been tired or careless>. The tide seems to be turning in our favour, but that may just be wishful thinking on my part. I often wonder at the wisdom of the higher ups. I suppose I shouldn't say such things here but I confess I am frustrated. Last night the moon was so bright (the rain finally having let up for a bit) my mates and I were reading the latest newspaper from England. Many weeks out of date, I might add. At any rate, we were gathered together seeing what was what and then the orders came to be ready to hop the bags. We were all flabbergasted to say the least. But orders are orders and over the top we went. Some of the lads didn't make it back, I'm afraid.

But all things considered the casualties could have been far worse.

This may not be the correct time to speak of this, but my heart dictates otherwise. Darling Annie, it is my dearest wish that as soon as I return to you I wish us to be married with all possible haste. Since we've been apart I feel I've been marking time and wasted years of our lives by being parted. If this suits you as well as it suits me, please reply with all haste, (well as hasty as the army mail service will allow ha ha). I look forward to your return post with hopeful heart.

The CO is shouting so I will close now.

With all good wishes
Pte George Richardson
Canadian Infantry (Eastern Ontario Regiment)
21st Btn

Annie refolded the smudged pages and tucked them into her bodice, close to her heart. She'd write to him this very evening after chores. If only she could snap her fingers and have George at her side. She would broach the idea of an early wedding once the war was over. She suspected Father would be in agreement, and Mother would be grateful her youngest daughter wouldn't disgrace her by dying an old maid. Annie giggled. And she must write to Peter, there had been a very short note from him. Nothing the censors even deemed necessary to black out. She grinned; the younger

Richardson boy was truly a man of few words. With a happy heart she skipped down the beaten path to bring the cows in to be milked. It was the first time she'd felt truly happy since the news of Steve's death. The pain was less fresh than it had been, but still a painful spike to her heart, striking at the most inopportune times. To her annoyance, she was prone to break into tears at the singing of certain songs, or hearing a turn of phrase that reminded her sharply of her brother. Nonsense, Annie. Steve wouldn't want you to brood over it. Let yourself be happy. She twirled in a circle, skirts floating around her. George wants to be married as much as I do. Annie hugged herself in glee before leaning on the pole gate and calling for the cows down in the meadow. In the distance the clack of the reaper in the wheat field carried on the evening air where the patient horses plodded back and forth across the grain field. Evan and Ivan followed behind stooking the long stalks to dry. Once the grain dried, Annie would be busy gathering wood and water for the steam powered threshing machine which would separate the grain from the chaff. Hauling the straw into the storage area of the large barn was Annie's job as well as Ivan's. Della and some others from the village promised to come and help. Della claimed it was a good excuse for a party, once the grain and straw was stored. Annie figured Frances would come as well, although nothing was official, she suspected her brother had more than a passing interest in the ex-nursing sister.

She called the cows again to hurry them as they meandered their way toward her. While she waited her thoughts turned to the war effort. The German offensives of the past spring had failed miserably which was, she supposed, a good thing. The newspapers reported the tide was swinging in the Allied's favour. Someplace called Amiens seemed to have been a major battle ground. She'd overheard Father speaking with some friends about the possibility of the Allieds mounting a counter-attack sometime soon to push the Germans back. I hope George and Peter are well away from that. Poor Peter, how many times did this make it that he'd been exposed to the mustard gas? Annie shook her head and opened the gate to let the cows into the barn yard and followed them into the barn where they filed into their stanchions.

Hooking the milking stool with one foot she settled herself and washed the first cow's udder with warm water and soap. She'd brought the pails down earlier before calling the cows. Drying the swollen udder she set a clean pail under it and set about filling the pail. Creamy hot milk pinged off the bottom of the bucket quickly turning to white froth as the level rose. Annie leaned her head on the Sue's brindled flank, her fingers automatically loosening to allow the teat to fill with fluid before closing thumb and forefinger to block the top of the teat then closing her fingers to flush the milk from the teat and begin the process all over again until all four teats were stripped and the udder was slack once more.

The full pail was covered with a clean cloth and set up on the shelf nearby. Giving Sue a pat on the side, Annie tossed her another fork of hay and moved on to the next animal. Sara regarded her with a sideways glance from her huge brown eye. The Jersey was Mother's pride and joy for the rich milk she produced. While Annie had to admit the creature was certainly lovely to look at with the fawn coloured coat and delicate dished face with the large liquid eyes, the cow was temperamental on the best of days. Righting the stool the beast had kicked over, Annie replaced it and turned to set a clean bucket underneath her. A well-aimed hoof sent the bucket in an arc to smack against the feed room.

"You devil! Keep it up and I'll rip that leg off and beat you with the wet end," she cursed. Glaring at the cow that blinked innocently at her, Annie stomped across the straw-strewn floor to retrieve the container. Sara moved restlessly when she approached and Annie gritted her teeth in resignation. Apparently it was going to be one of those days. The boys were all out in the fields so she'd have to manage this single-handedly. Setting the bucket down out of range of even the boldest cow kick, she took the sisal rope down from the hook on the feed room wall.

"There now you silly wench. Stand still now, just for a moment or I'll roast you for dinner, just you wait and see, you evil creature," Annie murmured in a soothing voice knowing the words didn't matter to the cow just the tone. Cheerfully informing Sara of the dire consequences awaiting her Annie ran a hand over the cow's back and neatly dropped the loop at the end of the rope where the animal would put a hind foot in it without realizing it. She leaned into the cow to encourage her to shift her weight and was rewarded by a hind hoof landing squarely where she intended. Drawing the loop tight she ran the end through the bell collar and wrapped it around a stout beam at the front of the stanchion. Throwing her weight into it, Annie tightened the tension until the rear leg was bent at the hock and the hoof off the ground. Knotting it securely with a quick release knot, she gave the cow a grim smile.

"Fine then, let's see you kick me now."

She pulled the stool up again and set a clean pail under the beast. Sara bellowed in frustration but there was no way to kick while standing on three legs. Annie went about the business of stripping the udder as quick as possible. She set the pail of thick creamy milk safely on the shelf before removing the hobble and throwing more hay into the manger.

"Not that you deserve it, you ungrateful creature."

The other cows were mild mannered and posed no further excitement. It took three trips from barn to house to transport the heavy pails to the back of the milk house. After being sure the separator was clean and not harbouring mouse turds or other foreign material, Annie spent the next hour separating the cream from the milk. The milk was poured into the stoneware crocks which she carted to the root cellar come cold shed, the cream, except for a container for their personal use, ended up in the shiny metal containers with the Eaton company name on them. She took those to the cold shed as well and placed them with the others. Evan would take them into the village to the train in order to send them off to the Timothy Eaton Company in Toronto, and collect the empty containers which would be sent back to them. While in the root cellar she checked the squat round stoneware tubs holding the butter. She selected one to take to the house as the crock in the icebox was next to empty. Eyeing the remaining tub, she sighed and added making butter to tomorrow's list of chores. It was pity she couldn't send butter through the post to George, he did love freshly churned butter so.

Closing the door securely, she deposited the fresh stoneware tub of butter in the icebox in the back mud room and then went back to the barn to turn the cows out again.

* * *

Next morning found her riding into Sprucedale next to Evan. Early morning light spilled like gold through the pines and littered the sandy road with dappled light. Annie breathed in the piney air and glanced upward where the arching canopy of maple, birch and oak branches let the blue sky peek through. Tinges of yellow on the birches and fiery orange on the maples and oaks contrasted with the rich array of green. Even though it was still August the edge to the early morning air was like an excitement in the blood and bespoke the arrival of autumn. Not too soon, she hoped, although in the Almaguin Highlands of Ontario Mother Nature sometimes decided to skip autumn altogether and winter could arrive in October, before Thanksgiving. Her heart was light with the unexpected trip to the village. Father needed some medical supplies and Mother sent a list of household items for Annie to pick up. A small pouch sat heavy in the pocket of her skirt, harvest money to bring Father's account up to date at Mulligan's General Store. A tiny thrill of excitement sent shivers over her skin. For once she would be the first to see the mail, there would be a packet of Father's newspapers, and maybe, just maybe, a letter from George. There had been nothing since the letter that arrived early in August. That wonderful missive where he'd declared himself. Annie hugged the memory to her. Nothing had been said to her parents yet, time enough for that once he was safe at home. They would tell her parents together and if they disagreed...well they'd cross that bridge when they came to it. A grim smile crossed her lips before she banished it. Mother was forever making comments to Hetty about despairing that Annie would ever have a man speak for her. Destined to die an old maid, Annie'd heard that old saw so often it was almost easy to ignore it now. Almost.

"You're awfully quiet this morning," Evan broke into her thoughts.

"Just thinking," she replied with a smile.

"I always think about Steve this time of year." He sighed, his eyes fixed on the horse's rump in front of him as the buckboard jolted over some washboard ruts. "Remember how he got so excited about bagging a moose? Or the time that old momma bear chased him?" Evan's eyes crinkled at the corners in amusement.

Annie laid a hand on his knee. "I do. You always had his back, even when he got in some bad scrapes he could have avoided."

"Except when it mattered. I didn't have his back then." He shook his head as if to clear it and then carried on as if he hadn't spoken. "Mind you, you girls made a big fuss over those two cubs he brought home."

"They were cute little things, but it was hard to enjoy bear steak with those two little beggars looking at me with those eyes."

"You always did have a soft heart, Annie."

"Oh, go on with you." She slapped his thigh lightly. "Who was it raised those baby raccoons when their mother got caught in that snare."

"Seemed the least I could after I killed their momma." His expression sobered. "A man gets to thinking a lot when he's laid up." He gestured to his missing right arm. "Sometimes all I can see if the faces of those soldiers I shot. Some of 'em didn't look much older than Ivan, for God's sake."

"Evan," Annie tried to soothe him, change the subject but it was like he didn't hear her.

"You don't know what it was like, Annie. And I'm right glad you don't. But when they gave the order, we just went. Up over the top, slippin' and slidin' in the mud and the blood, runnin' and shooting…It weren't so bad when you couldn't see their faces, just fire blind and hope to hell nobody hit you. But God…" He tucked the lines under his thigh and rubbed his hand roughly over his face. "When they were right there, shooting at you and you knew it was them or you; kill or be killed, and their faces…scared as you were, but no more choice than us poor bastards…" Evan retrieved the reins from under his leg and clucked to the horse. "Get along there, you."

"Evan, I'm sorry. If there's anything I can do…"

"There isn't anything anyone can do, Annie. I just wish I could get it out of my head."

"Does it help to talk about it? I can listen if you want?" she offered.

He nudged her with his thigh. "Thanks, sis. I already said more than I should, unless you've experienced it you can't begin to imagine what it was like. What it's still like for those poor bastards still over there."

"What about Frances, can you talk to her?"

"Aye, I can. And it helps, helps us both. I've had men die by my hand, but Frances…she's had men die under her hand and nothing she could do to help them. Of the two of us, I think her burden is harder to bear than mine."

"I'm glad you can talk to someone, then."

"Here we are. You run along to Mulligans while I take care of the freight." He halted the wagon at the station.

Annie jumped down from the buckboard, careful her skirts didn't catch on the brake or the wheel hub. In no time she settled Father's account and gathered the sundry items on her list. She saved the post for last, savouring the anticipation and staving off disappointment if there were no letters for her.

"Any post, Mrs. Mulligan?" She stowed the household items in the satchel she'd brought and carefully packed the medical supplies in another.

"I do believe there is, Annabelle. Just let me go look." Mrs. Mulligan bustled away.

Annie tapped her foot and glanced out the window toward the train station. The buckboard was still pulled up to the platform so Evan must still be exchanging the full cream containers for the empties. Her gaze wandered over the dry goods and came to rest on a bolt of cream coloured linen. Now wouldn't that make a nice wedding dress? She had no need of silk and lace, linen would do just fine. Practical and easy to alter so she could wear it again.

"Here we are, dear. Mister Baldwin's newspapers all the way from Toronto and London. My stars, imagine where those papers have travelled and myself never going any further than North Bay." She shook her head and placed the rolled up newspapers on the counter. "And some letters, I see. One from your sister down in Trenton and some others."

"Thanks." Annie gathered the bundle of letters and shoved them in with the papers. One of the envelopes peeking out was from overseas but who it was from wasn't clear. Please, please, let it be from George. Please. She crossed her fingers inside her skirt pocket before taking the satchels from the counter and heading for the door.

"Oh, there you are. Almost done?" Evan appeared in the entryway, his expression guarded.

"Yes, I was just coming." She took his arm and steered him out the door. "What's wrong? You look awful." She peered up at her brother.

"Nothing." He shook his head.

"Doesn't look like nothing." Annie steered him over to the bench set against the wall by the door. "Is it Frances?"

"No...yes...but that's..."

Annie stood up. "I'll go find Della, she'll know what's going on."

Evan caught her arm. "Don't, Annie. Frances is sick in bed with malaria. Doc Lewen is looking after her. She'll be fine once this bout passes."

"Where in heaven's name did she get malaria? I've heard Father mention it, but…"

"She nursed in Italy. A lot of the lads caught it there. They treat it with quinine, but it never goes away apparently. Just comes and goes."

"That's horrible. But if it isn't Frances, then what is it, Evan?" She sank down beside him.

He leaned over, elbows resting on his knees and his face in his hands. "It's hard to talk about it, Annie. Don't you understand?"

"Sometimes talking about it helps, Evan," she said, rubbing his back with a gentle hand.

He drew a quivering breath and raised his head a bit. "Not here, too many nosey parkers." Evan rose and strode toward the waiting buckboard. Elsie, the pretty palomino Father bought to please Mother tossed her head with impatience and stamped at the flies plaguing her.

Her brother was silent until they passed out of the sunlight and entered the confines of the bush crowding both sides of the sandy road. Dust and flies danced in the sunbeams spearing through the canopy. The air in the thickest part of the bush always seemed to take on a greenish tint to Annie's eyes. She waited for Evan to speak.

"The boys at the train were talkin' about the war. Sounds like there was a big push the beginning of August. They've never been overseas, they have no idea what it's like. Not all glory and pushing the dirty Huns back for

King and Country. Oh no, it's cold and wet and or hot and wet, poison gas and terrible food. It's all so senseless, Annie. All the killing, I can't get their faces out of my head." He shuddered and closed his eyes. "It's the ones you kill face to face that haunts you, not the faceless ones the shells blow to bits or the ones you never see. And then there's your mates, splattered all over everything when a whiz bang hits. Just the whine and then no time to hide, if there was even a place to hide, which there isn't. It's going to sleep scared out of your mind and waking up the same. Those boys back there, they just don't understand. They've never had to listen to their mates lying in mud and blood in no man's land, caught in the wire, bleeding to death, calling for their mothers, crying for help and you stuck in the trench under orders not to go to them."

"I'm sorry, Evan. I wish there was something I could do to help you." Annie leaned against his shoulder. "You're safe now, though. That's a blessing." It frightened her that he didn't seem to realize he'd talked about the same things on the ride into the village.

"Is it?" He looked down at her desolation etched on his face. "It's guilty I feel for not still being over there fighting with those poor buggers. PBI they called us, Poor Bloody Infantry, and by God that's what we were."

"You were injured, Evan. That's not your fault," Annie began.

"Not my fault, no. But to my dishonour I was almost glad when it happened. Either I'd die or I'd get to go to Blighty. Either way I was out of it, and those poor lads I left behind weren't…" his voice trailed off.

Annie let him be alone with his thoughts, turning over his words in her mind. Her stomach roiled at the images his tale evoked in her mind. Was that how Steve died? The newspaper reports made it sound so cut and dried when reporting casualties. Somehow Annie always assumed getting killed involved getting shot and dropping dead. Not slowly bleeding to death crying for help that never came. She hugged her arms around her. Her George was still there, somehow still safe, and Peter too. She crossed fingers on both hands in the hope their luck still held.

Evan was silent the rest of the drive home, he halted Elsie by the house long enough for Annie to alight. Then he turned her toward the barn. "Please tell Mother I won't be in for supper," he called back over his shoulder.

Annie stood on the top step and watched him go toward the barn. He'd take care of the horse and then no doubt go on one of his solo rambles down to the shores of Doe Lake and into the bush. The flies were still fierce but Annie reckoned her brother would hardly notice them.

Giving him one last worried glance, she hurried into the house to deliver the mail to Father's study. She kept out the letters addressed to her. Three of them, she realized with a thrill. One from Peter, she flipped through them, one from the middle Foley boy and, thank goodness, one from George. Annie slid them into her skirt pocket to read later. Mother's summons drew her to the kitchen where she was kept too busy to do more than smile over her good fortune to receive three letters in one day.

* * *

Annie finished the milking by herself in jig time. Evan was still off on his wander and she didn't begrudge him the time. It meant she could steal a few precious moments to read her letters in the privacy of the barn before lugging the milk and cream to the milk house. She tore open Ed Foley's first. It was brief, thanking her for the package with thick socks and a tin of biscuits. She frowned in consternation at the x and o he'd contrived to add to his signature. While she was fond of Ed, that was as far as it went. She'd have to be sure he realized that, Annie had no intention of letting him have hope in that direction.

Peter's next

July 16, 1918
Dear Annie,
Well, I've done ended up in a convalescent home again. I must have more lives than a cat. ha ha. We were setting up a field hospital near

207

the front lines and wham Bertha (that's a 1200 lb shell) hit some distance off. The concussion of its passing and impact however affect a much larger area. My mate and I were buried under the rubble for over 48 hours before our boys heard us hollering and dug us out. I'm a little banged up, but okay. Having trouble catching me breath 'cause I got gassed again, but the docs say I'll be right as rain soon.

Hoping you are keeping well. You can write to this address and if I've gone back they'll forward it on to me.

Your Friend,
Sapper Peter Richardson
788629
9th Canadian Rail Troops

Annie folded the fragile sheet and tucked it between her leg and the milking stool she'd drawn up against the feed room wall. She glanced out the open double doors of the barn to judge the angle of the sun. Still time to read George's at least once. She held the letter for moment, savouring the anticipation of learning the contents. Running a finger over the bold scrawl of her name brought a sense of comfort, almost as if she could touch him and feel him near.

With careful fingers she opened the thin sheet

August 2, 1918
Dearest Annie,

This must of necessity be short. The company is preparing to move, where I don't know and of course I couldn't tell you even if I did. But something big is in the offing. I can feel it. It may be some time before I can write to you again, but know you are ever in my thoughts and dreams. I have a favour I need to ask of you. If the unthinkable happens and I don't come home for some reason, I need to know you'll look after Peter for me. We're the only family we have, and I can't stand the thought of him being alone in the world. It eases my heart to know you'll honour my wishes, even without hearing from you, I know this.

Knowing you wait for me is the only thing that keeps me from going crackers in the midst of this insanity. I have the token you sent me tucked in the Bible in my breast pocket over my heart, along with your lock of hair, so I feel you are ever nearby watching over me. I echo the sentiments of your last letter, that this war be over soon. From your lips to God's ears.

I dare to sign myself

Your devoted fiancé

Pte George Richardson

Canadian Infantry (Eastern Ontario Regiment)

21st Btn

Annie held the crackling paper to her lips. It smelled of dried damp and musty, the page splotched with old water marks and perhaps mud. She hoped it was only mud. His letter seemed to bear out what Evan overheard at the

209

train station and the brief glance she'd managed at the headlines of Father's newspapers. Surely, the war must end soon; they couldn't go on fighting forever, could they? His words stuck starkly in her mind. Of course she'd look out for Peter. Both of them would. When George came home. Standing, she tucked the letters into her pocket and began lugging the heavy milk pails to the milk shed to be separated.

Chapter Fifteen

September 1918 drew to a close and October rolled along. Thanksgiving was a quiet affair owing to the war shortages and Mother sending food to friends in England. The woods were ablaze with the orange-red torches of the sugar maples, contrasting with the yellow flame of the larch and birch. Overhead, skeins of geese stitched the sky from dawn to dusk. The cacophony of their honking filling Annie's ears from morning til night. She loved to steal a few moments at dusk when the chores were done to walk down to Doe Lake near Gordon Dean's cottages and join the Finlanders watching the seemingly never ending flocks of geese coming in to settle for the night. Some nights she was lucky enough to see white snow geese, whistling swans and the massive tundra swans who dwarfed the Canada Geese. The Canadas were a good size, she knew intimately from plucking and cleaning the ones Father and Evan brought back from their hunting forays.

The birds mated for life, and it was a sore spot for Annie that such a bond could be so casually broken. But her practical side reminded her she also liked to eat, and without the bounty of the bush it would be a long hungry winter. So, she apologized while she plucked and cleaned the big birds. Even though it made no difference to the creature under her hands, it made her feel better. Evan had changed since he came home from the war. Where before he used to enjoy hunting as much as the next man, now he often wandered off on his own after returning with the kill. Once, Annie found him turning his stomach inside out behind the wood shed. She'd hesitated and finally decided it was best to leave him alone. No man wanted his little sister to see him in such a state.

How much would George be changed when he came home? She supposed she should be expecting he would be plagued by the same kind of horrible memories her brother was. Annie straightened her shoulders. Well, she would just help him deal with them; she felt she understood a little bit of what he would undoubtedly go through from observing Evan and easing him from the throes of his nightmares. I wonder if that's what is keeping him from asking Frances to marry him? I'm certain he has strong feelings for her, and I know from Della that she feels the same. They're both so broken from what they experienced overseas, I wonder if they'll ever feel safe enough to allow themselves to be happy. Now there was a depressing thought. She pushed it from her mind and got on with living and waiting for the war to finally end.

* * *

The third week of October came and went with no word from George. Even given the vagrancies of the overseas post, she had expected to hear something by the end of September. Annie slapped the lines on Elsie's tawny haunches, the mare already thickening her coat in preparation for the coming winter. Leaves crunched under the buckboard wheels sending a dry crisp scent into the air to mingle with the dust. The fall rains were late this year and it looked like they were set to enjoy an open fall. By this time some years the snow had already flown. Above her the west wind whirled more leaves from the branches sending them cascading down around her. She smiled and reached out to catch one, admiring the brilliant red of the maple leaf.

Evan was feeling poorly this day so Annie had set off to Sprucedale to deliver the cream and fetch the mail. The blaze of colour around her lifted her spirits and she broke into song, raising her voice in one of her favourite hymns, she let the last notes of Onward Christian Soldiers linger in the air as she drove into the outskirts of the village. It was only the work of a few minutes to exchange the full cream cans for the returning empties. With a cheery wave, Annie stepped on the wheel hub and settled on the seat of the buckboard. After exchanging pleasantries with Mrs. Mulligan and gathering up the mail she returned to where Elsie waited patiently. She took a moment to shuffle through newspapers and other items. Yes! There was a letter for her. Her excitement dimmed a bit when she realized it was from Peter and not George. But it was news at least after such a long silence. Annie was tempted to read it then and there, but Father was expecting the buckboard back and she wanted to stop and have a word with Della and Frances while she was in the village. She shoved the letter in the pocket of her sweater and tucked the tails of her shawl into her belt. Time for that later, for now a little match making was in order. Evan wouldn't thank her for the interference, but Annie was certain she knew what was best for both her brother and Frances. Even young Ivan was starting to make cow's eyes at some of the village girls. She grinned; get Evan settled first, then she could turn her attention to Ivan.

Spending a quarter of an hour consulting with Della, they managed to convince Frances the two girls should come out to the Baldwin farm on Sunday afternoon for tea. Annie promised Della she'd make sure Evan was about. Giggling the two girls embraced before Annie mounted the wagon and waved farewell.

It wasn't until later that night Annie had a chance to open Peter's letter. The words wavered in the lamp light. She forced herself to read it twice before letting it lie in her lap, eyes staring blankly at the night pressed against the window.

Dear Annie,

There is no easy way to say this. I have no way of knowing if Mister Miller has contacted you or not, so I thought I should write to you as soon as I could.

Here, she stopped and pressed a hand to her chest. What on earth would Mister Miller be writing to her for? Her heart beat erratically against her palm. She dropped her eyes to the paper.

Since I last wrote you I have returned to active duty, albeit a little worse for wear. Just before I left the convalescent home I received a message from George's captain.

The writing ended in an ink splotch before continuing on a new line.

I'm sorry, Annie. I am finding this very hard to write. George's company was engaged in the big push at Amiens in the beginning of August. From what I can find out, the weather was very bad and prevented the backup that should have supported the infantry. It was near the little town of Marcelcave, maybe you've read accounts of the battle in the newspaper by now? It was a great victory for the Allieds.

Annie clenched her fingers in the quilt. "What aren't you telling me, Peter? George must have been injured, that's it and he just doesn't know how to tell me," she whispered.

Annie, I'm so sorry. George was one of the first over the top if the information I have is true. The fighting was fierce and at first he was listed as Missing in Action.

Her heart tripped in her chest and she swallowed hard. Like Steve, like Steve. No, not like Steve. George is fine, he has to be.

I just got official word today that my brother was killed in action on the morning of 8th August, 1918. It still doesn't seem quite real and I regret the time it will take for this letter to reach you. I'm not sure if you're aware of this, but George made me vow to take care of you if something happened to him. He worried that he shouldn't have made you a promise before enlisting but no one imagined the war would last this long. It was a cause of unrest to him that you were waiting for him and would most likely be considered an old maid if he didn't return owing to the fact you discouraged interest from other men.

I have a confession to make, which may seem ill conceived at this point in time. I have always admired you but put my own feelings aside when it was so apparent how you and my brother felt for each other. I am hoping that with time, you will come to feel some affection for me, as I mean to live up to my promise to my brother.

I will understand if you don't feel disposed to replying in the near future. In the event I don't hear, once the war is over (which I pray will be soon) I am headed to British Columbia with a couple of my mates who assure me there will be work for us, one of their uncles being a foreman at Fraser Mills. My address there is below and I will be in touch once things are settled. For the foreseeable future I will be here defending King and Country.

In closing, I regret being the bearer of such sad news, please know I share in your grief. I have lost my only brother and am quite alone in the world, apart from yourself.

With much admiration and regret
Sapper Peter Richardson
788629
9th Canadian Rail Troops

She forced herself to read it twice before letting it lie in her lap, eyes staring blankly at the night pressed against the window. Her dreams lay in shatters around her, scattered like the diamond points of the stars tossed across the ebony sky. George couldn't be dead, he just couldn't. Wouldn't she have known? Felt something? Mother always said I was cursed with the Second Sight, a legacy of her Scottish heritage and Father's Irish. Why didn't I feel something? At first the hurt was too deep to allow the tears to come. Bottled up inside her, it cramped her limbs and hobbled her thoughts. Evan's words about his mates lying in the mud bleeding to death and crying for help plunged her into an almost trance. Images, blurred and erratic skipped across her inner eye, pain, blood, anguish and hopelessness swept over her. Dear God, let it have been quick. If it had to happen, let it have been quick. No solace in any official notice, according to Evan, they always said it was quick and how the loved one died a hero.

Even if that was the farthest thing from the truth.

George was dead, killed in action on some God Forsaken foreign battle field, alone. It was more than she could bear. Brave. Strong. I need to be strong for George. He'd want me to be strong. Annie bit her lip and sat up straighter. She could do this. She could. There was Peter to think about, yes, think about Peter. Poor lad must be heartbroken, the brothers were so close. Annie hugged the knowledge she'd written back to George by return post assuring him of her promise to look out for Peter. Please let that letter have reached him before whatever happened…well…happened. She spent the night sitting cross-legged and dried-eyed in her bed, letter in her lap and her shawl pulled tight around her shoulders.

The sky was still dark when she heard Evan stirring in the kitchen below. Mechanically, she dressed, after smoothing the letter and placing it in the pages of the Bible by her bed. She went about the usual morning chores of stoking the fire in the cook stove. Evan had already made tea, but not built the fire under the wider part of the stove. Methodically, she sliced bacon off the side in the icebox. Father slaughtered a hog only a week ago, so there was plenty of fresh meat.

Her brother went off to feed the animals and throw down hay from the loft. Annie turned the rashers of bacon and scrambled a half-dozen eggs in the grease when the meat was done. Sliding the plate into the warming oven, she made a fresh pot of tea and set it on the trivet on the cast iron stove top. Pulling on her coat and stomping into her boots, she headed off to do the morning milking.

"Annabelle!" Father's voice hailed her from the kitchen as she entered the mudroom with a pail of fresh milk in each hand. She sighed and set them down. Whatever did he want this early in the morning and her with the cheese still to make.

"Yes, Father." She hung her bonnet and coat on a hook, kicked off her barn shoes and smoothed her hair before slipping on her house shoes. Pausing, she took a deep breath before pushing open the door.

He sat at the kitchen table across from Mother holding a letter in his hand, the London papers spread out before him. The expression on his face puzzled her, a mix between vexation and sympathy.

"Yes?" She moved toward the stove intending to fetch the plate of bacon and eggs to the table. "Would you like me to toast some bread? Fry up some taters?"

"Leave that for now, Annabelle. Come sit down," Father commanded.

A thread of trepidation skewered through her. What is going on here? She crossed the floor and sat on the edge of a chair.

"What do you know about this?" Father waved the papers in his hand.

"I'm sorry?" Annie frowned. "What do I know about what?"

"I have a letter and a telegram which has taken a while to reach me." He paused and regarded her thoughtfully. "The telegram is to inform me that George Richardson was killed in action. The letter is from his brother Peter, informing me of the same and in the same breath asking for your hand in marriage. Some promise he made to his dead brother. What do you know of this?"

"I had a letter from Peter that arrived yesterday informing me of George's death." She was proud her voice didn't break. "Why did the telegram take so long and why in heaven's name was it sent to you?"

Father heaved a long sigh. "It seems your friend listed me as his next of kin, but didn't give the army our new address. This telegram was sent first to Renfrew, then to Eganville and finally routed here."

"Oh," Annie's voice was faint.

"I gather you have, I beg your pardon, had, an understanding with George Richardson before he enlisted and went overseas." Father fixed her with a gimlet eye.

"That's true. I just found out last night he isn't coming home." She blinked hard and willed back the tears stinging the inside of her nose.

"And what of this proposal from the younger Richardson boy? What do you know of this?"

Annie glanced at her mother, who refused to meet her eye and poured more tea into her cup, stirring in sugar with a small silver spoon.

"The first I heard of it was in his letter which I received only last night. I did promise George that I'd look out for Peter if anything happened to him and he didn't come home. But marriage...?"

"I see." Father pursed his lips and tapped a long finger on the table regarding her as he might a horse or cow he was considering purchasing. "I see," he repeated. "And what do you think of this idea, Annabelle?"

"Why I've barely had time to accept that George isn't coming home. I haven't given the other matter much thought," she admitted. Marry Peter? Well, I suppose I could do worse.

"I've been concerned about your social standing in the community for a while now. I've had certain gentlemen express, shall we say an interest, in you, but you've rebuffed them all. If you keep on this way you're going to end up an old maid. Why Hetty was saying just the other day how you were rude to Clarence's brother when he asked you to dinner—"

"Hetty!" Annie surged to her feet. "What does Hetty have to say about my private life?" Anger flared through her, lending her courage to speak her mind. "I'd sooner die an old maid than have anything to do with that dry stick of a man, Frederick Lucas. For that matter, what Hetty sees in that husband of hers is beyond me, but that's her business."

"Sit down, Annabelle. And mind your tongue when you speak to me," Father commanded her. "Sit!"

Reluctantly, she sat. "Yes, Father."

"Now, your mother and I have spoken this morning, and all in all, we are of the mind that I shall respond to Mister Peter Richardson's letter in a positive manner." He held up a hand to forestall her protest when she opened her mouth. "Although, he is admittedly below our social standing, he has acquitted himself admirably in the defense of King and Country. And given your rebuttal of any eligible male in the vicinity, your prospects are, to say the least, limited. We feel it is in your best interest to accept this proposal. We must make the best of a bad situation. I will respond post haste with an affirmative, and then we can iron out the details once the boy returns to Canada."

"Do I get a say in this?" Annie glared at her father.

"Not really, no. You are unmarried and living under my roof and protection, so no. You have no say." Father picked up the newspaper signalling the end of the conversation.

Annie knew better than to push the situation when he was in that mood. She'd hadn't had time to even think clearly about Peter's idea. And, she did promise George to look after his brother. In silence she got the bacon and eggs from the warming oven and filled a plate for her parents and then added two for Evan and Ivan when they came through the door after chores.

Taking a handful of biscuits from the larder, she scurried out the door.

"Annie! Aren't you going to have breakfast?" Ivan called after her.

"Leave her be," Father's voice followed her.

She walked stiff-legged toward the barn. Once there, she broke into a run and raced pell mell down the lane toward Doe Lake. The breath burned in her lungs and her vision blurred with unshed tears. Her bare feet hit the soft sand of the Sprucedale Road then she was past it and pelting down the track leading to Dean's cottages. Just before she reached the buildings Annie angled off to the left following a deer path to a granite promontory shaded by a stand of white pine. She dropped to her knees in the soft bed of shed needles, hands digging into forest loam. White lights flared before her eyes while she fought for breath, forcing her tight muscles to draw oxygen into her starving lungs. Finally, her emotions settled, having run their course for the moment. She had no idea how long she'd laid on the forest floor; long enough to be stiff and cold. Annie crawled from the piney shade out onto the sun warmed granite out crop overlooking the mirror still water of the large lake.

Willing herself not to think, not to feel, Annie tracked the journey of the sun across the cerulean blue October sky. She squinted at its position and reckoned it was just past noon. Time seemed to have no meaning at the moment. The air cooled as the afternoon waned, forcing her to attend to the needs of her body. At some point, she'd have to return to the house. Face the music, so to speak. She sighed deeply and gave in to the anguish battering to be set free. Later, how much later she wasn't sure, Annie's tears of grief subsided and she was left with a terrible emptiness where the anger and grief had resided. *How am I to go on? All the dreams, dead and gone, with George. Should I go along with it and marry Peter? What does it matter? What does anything matter? I suppose I must marry someone, so why not Peter. I'll sleep on it, maybe things will be clearer in the morning.*

"Are you well?" The man's voice speaking broken English startled her to her feet.

"What? Oh, hello, Aapeli. On your way home from work are you?"

The tall broad shouldered Finlander nodded. "You alright? You sure?" His gaze took in her rumpled clothing and dishevelled hair. "You no hurt?" Aapeli glanced around, looking for a possible assailant, she supposed.

"I'm fine, Aapeli," she assured him. "I just received some bad news, is all."

The big man set down his lunch container and sat cross-legged on the stone looking out over the lake where the sun turned the waters to molten gold. "You come sit. Tell Aapeli. Grief shared is grief halved." He patted the warm granite at his side.

Annie joined him, watching the sunset spread across the lake and surrounding bush. It was so very beautiful it seemed unfair such wonder should exist in a world that saw fit to take George from her. They sat in companionable silence while the evening wind stirred the pine boughs behind them. She'd often spoken with Aapeli and his wife Ana when running errands for Father. The Finlanders came up to the house whenever someone was injured or ill, and Annie was often pressed into service to deliver Father's potions and medicines. A small community lived in the cottages Gordon Dean owned clustered on the shores of the lake. Gentle waves lapped at the sandy beach in front of the small cabins. Already smoke drifted from the chimneys.

Annie poured her heart out to the silent man beside her. Aapeli was one her favourites, he often helped her doctor wild creatures she found in the bush. Nothing dangerous of course, but orphaned raccoons and squirrels, baby rabbits. The big man had a heart as big as his girth.

When she finally fell silent, Annie felt marginally better, although no less confused about how to go forward.

"You love him, this soldier who comes no more?" The tone was soft, his gaze never leaving the play of light on the lake.

"I did, I do." She sniffed and wiped her nose on the hem of her skirt.

"And this brother of his, the one who asks for your hand? What feel you for him?"

225

"I don't know! That's more than half the problem," she cried, throwing up her hands. "I've known him as long as I've known George. He's closer to my age than his brother, and of course I feel affection for him. But enough to marry him? Spend my life with him?"

"What of this promise you spoke of? This Peter, he made promise too?"

"Yes, I suppose he did," Annie admitted. Tipping her head to the side, she looked up at him. "What would you do, Aapeli? What would you do?"

"Me? I am simple man. I would feel honour to keep promise made to dead man." He shrugged. "But that is me." He got to his feet and offered Annie a hand up. "I go now, Ana will worry if I late come home."

Annie took the proffered hand and scrambled to her feet. "Yes, don't cause Ana any worry on my account. Thank you for listening, my friend."

The big Finlander smiled at her and ruffled her hair. In her haste, she'd forgotten to take her bonnet from the hook in the back room. "You go too, dark coming. You alright home alone?"

Annie nodded and Aapeli disappeared into the gloom under the pines. The light was fading and Annie hurried her steps back to the track leading toward the Sprucedale Road. All manner of hunters were out once the dark fell under the trees. None of them would mean her any harm unless she stumbled across them, but she had no wish to run into a bear, or a pack of

226

coyotes or wolves. By the time she reached the barn gate the sun was behind the trees.

Entering the barn, she was surprised to see the milking was already done. Evan or Ivan must have taken care of it for her. Pulling the double doors shut again she walked up the path toward the house.

Annie went about the motions of helping with supper and the clearing up afterward. Outwardly calm, or at least she hoped that was the case, her emotions were in turmoil. Nothing would ever fill the void left by George's death, of that she was sure. She was fond of Peter, but was fondness strong enough to build a life on? For the life of her, Annie couldn't come to a decision. One part of her wanted to crawl into a hole and die; another part thought living out her days as a spinster would be just fine. But, that would mean living under Father's roof and she was pretty sure if she didn't go along with his demand she take Peter up on his offer her life would be a living hell. Not to mention Hetty needling her every chance she got. The thought of Hetty distracted her for a moment. Rotha's last letter from Trenton included the information she had met a certain young man who more than caught her fancy. Perhaps there would be another Baldwin wedding to distract her parents, other than Annie's, of course. It didn't look as if Evan and Frances had any immediate plans at the moment.

She fell into bed exhausted and barely remembered pulling the quilts up. Instead of restful sleep, Annie walked in a green wood, frothy white apple and choke cherry blossoms gleaming against the brilliant spring leaves. The earth under her bare feet was warmish and gave off a pleasant loamy scent. Everything was so tactile and alive; it was unlike a normal dream. Annie recognized the strange feeling of a sending or as her grandmother explained, a vision of sorts brought on by the Second Sight.

"Annie."

She whirled around at the sound of her name. "George!" She threw herself into his arms. He was solid and real, his hand stroked her hair, his lips warm on hers. Only his eyes were different when she drew back to gaze at his face. They were the same warm grey, but shadows lay behind them giving him a haunted look.

"Annie, God I miss you." His arms tightened around her.

"Why are you here? I must be dreaming." Annie moved with him to sit on a mossy stump, his arms around her shoulders. His heart beat under her hand where it rested on his chest. How can that be? Oh, I don't care. Don't spoil this by trying to figure it out. You know it can't last long.

George stirred and tipped her face up toward his. "I came to remind you of your promise. I need to know Peter will be cared for. You can make him happy. He's always been in love with you. He's my little brother and I've always done my best to see him right. Will you honour your pledge to me? Please, dearest Annie. I can't rest until I know Peter is settled."

Tears sprang to her eyes and she blinked hard. "It's so hard, George. To go on, you know? I'm just going through the motions of living, but there's just this huge empty pit where my heart and my joy used to be."

"I know, Annie. I know. It's unfair of me to ask it of you." He stroked her hair, tangling his fingers in the unbound strands.

Where is my bonnet? The random thought surprised her.

"I've imagined you like this, your hair around your shoulders, all soft against me. I dreamed of it lying in the filth and mud in the trenches. We used to talk of our sweethearts, the lads and me. You wouldn't believe how many of the poor buggers got Dear John letters from home. I wonder if those girls realized how it ripped the heart out of the boys who got them. One of my mates went crazy, kept throwing himself over the bags and begging Fritz to shoot him. They never did then. Alf went down right next to me when I was hit; the last thing I heard was him saying 'At last.' I tried to live, Annie. I really did, but it was wet with thick pea soup fog, and I was hit more than once." He paused. "It's true you know, what they say. It doesn't hurt a first, just a numbness. Then the blood runs hot, then it feels cold, so cold. Too cold, too much blood…" His voice faded.

"George! Don't go. Not yet!" Annie clutched at his shoulders.

He raised his head. "No, not yet. I need your promise. Promise me you'll marry Peter, do your best to make him happy. Can you do that for me, Annie? Please?" His form wavered in the sweet green air.

"Yes! Yes, I'll do it. For you, I'll never stop loving you, but I promise to do my best to make Peter happy. Give us both a good life."

"Thank you, dearest." The flesh under her hands became insubstantial, his face transparent. "I'll wait for you, when the time comes, I'll be there waiting for you. Til then, Annie." His lips brushed hers and then she was left with nothing but the scent of apple blossoms.

She woke with a start, bolt upright with the quilt clutched to her chest, eyes searching the dark for a familiar face. The scent of apple blossoms clung to her hair.

Chapter Sixteen

Between 510 and 520 a.m. on a foggy French morning in railway car Number 2419 D on a siding in the Forest of Compiegne some 37 miles north of Paris, the Armistice was signed. Present in the rail car were from France, the Supreme Commander of the Allied Armies, Ferdinand Foch, and General Maxime Weygard. Representing Britain British Naval Officer Captain Jack Marriott, Naval Officers Rear Admiral George Hope, and First Sea Admiral Sir Rosslyn Wemyss. The German delegation was led by politician and official government representative Matthais Erzberger, he was accompanied by Admiral Ernst Vonselow, and German Count Alfred Von Obendorff. The document was signed by F. Foch, R.E. Wemyss, Erzberger, A. Oberndorff, Winterfeldt, and Vonselow.

The official cease fire, the end of the war to end all wars, was agreed upon to occur on the 11th hour of the 11th day of November, 1918.

Annie slept fitfully through the night of November 10, 1918, unknowing of the fact that at 11 o'clock Eastern Time on that date, the war was declared over.

* * *

"Father, Father!" Evan pulled Elsie up at the front steps and jumped down from the buckboard seat. Ivan stood on the sacks of feed in the wagon bed whooping at the top of his lungs.

Annie left the milk pails and hurried out of the barn toward the house. What in the world is going on? Evan hasn't been this excited since I can't remember when. And what's gotten into Ivan. Mother will scold him for sure for acting like a hooligan. She broke into a run and arrived breathless just as her parents stepped out of the house.

"Evan, what is all this nonsense?" Father demanded.

Instead of answering, Evan grabbed Annie with his good arm and danced her around in an impromptu jig. Giving her a final spin, he stopped.

"It's over! The war is over! I got the news when I picked up the mail! It's over! Thank God."

"Are you sure?" Father frowned.

Annie's legs threatened to give out and deposit her in a heap. She disengaged herself from her brother and sat on the bottom step, attempting to gather her scattered thoughts. It's over? Oh George, you almost made it. Just another three months and you'd have been coming home. Bitterness rose in her throat. She should be happy for the men and boys who would be coming home, but somehow just right this moment it was a struggle. Evan's voice penetrated the fog in her brain.

"Yes, it's official. The Germans signed the agreement around five in the morning French time, so last night our time. I can hardly believe it. The fighting is supposed to stop at eleven a.m." He glanced at his watch. "Which means it's already done. That would have made it five in the morning here. Ivan, you eejit, quit screeching would you?" Evan hauled his younger brother off the wagon and cuffed him good naturedly on the ear.

"Mister Mulligan said he heard David Lloyd the British Prime Minister announced it on the steps of Number Ten Downing Street. We should unload the feed and head back into the village. They're celebrating in the street. It's bedlam, everyone's shouting and dancing, the Mulligans are giving out candy to all the kids. C'mon, Ivan. Let's get this unloaded. I want to go find Frances."

Evan led Elsie toward the barn, followed by Ivan. I should go get the milk. The abstract thought failed to spur her into motion. Her limbs seemed stuck in thick clay, unmoving in spite of her intention to get to her feet. Shaking her head to clear it, Annie pushed to her feet and trailed after her brothers. Peter would be coming home. Not George, though. No, he was being buried in some foreign grave yard, far from home and no chance of Annie every seeing his grave. Peter's last letter said he'd managed to get in touch with someone and found out George was buried near some place called Villers-Bretonneux. Lord, she couldn't even pronounce it. Appropriately, she thought grimly, the grave yard was named Crucifix Corner Cemetery.

Working without really thinking about what her body was doing, Annie helped unload the feed and then carried the milk pails up to the house. It would have to be separated and then stored in the cold cellar before she could go anywhere. Evan's voice echoed out the open back door of the house urging her parents to hurry and chivvying Ivan. He was certainly in a hurry to get to the village. Maybe the war ending would spur him to act on his feelings and ask Frances to marry him finally. Lord knew the whole village and surrounding area was aware the two of them only had eyes for each other.

"C'mon, Annie. Hurry up!" Ivan stuck his head into the milk house.

"You all go on without me. I need to finish up with the milk. I can ride one of the plow horses into the village when I'm done. Sarge is broke to ride. Tell them to go and I'll catch up with everyone in a bit."

Ivan regarded her with an odd expression and shrugged. The sound of his feet thundering over the floor boards reached her even across the yard. She needed time alone to figure out how she felt. Glad the fighting was over, of course. But what did it mean for her personally? Peter would be coming back and expecting her to marry him. Annie supposed she did need to marry someone, and if that was so, then Peter was the best of the lot in her opinion. She paused in the process of tipping cream in to a clean can. The crazy dream, the Sight, she was sure of it. She'd promised George she'd take care of his brother. Annie sighed and rested her head on one of the spouts of the cream separator. It would be enough to base a life on, wouldn't it? They both loved George, and it seemed they'd both promised to look out for the other. It would be enough, it had to be.

* * *

For some reason, Annie thought since the fighting was over the troops would be coming home by the end of the year. The newspaper reports soon disabused her of this notion. Although the Armistice was signed on November 11th, 1918, it wasn't really in effect until the Treaty of Versailles was signed in the end of June, 1919. It seemed a long drawn out process to her. Now she'd made up her mind to marry Peter, she just wanted to get on with it.

The first Armistice lasted from November 11 to December 13, 1918. Then there was a prolongation from December 13, 1918 to January 16, 1919. Then a second prolongation, followed by a third that lasted past the signing of the Treaty of Versailles until January 10, 1920 when peace was finely ratified at four-fifteen p.m. French time.

Annie spent the time helping Frances and Della prepare for Frances and Evan's wedding.

Evan and Frances finally came to an agreement and neither wanted to wait any longer than was necessary. She sewed on her own trousseau along with Frances'. Between the girls they turned out delicate undergarments, hemmed bed linens, embroidered pillow cases and towels. It made her blush to work the entwined initials of A and P on hand towels and pillowcases. Annie's stomach twisted oddly when they began to work on baby clothes and cutting and hemming flannel diapers. Somehow it made everything so startlingly clear. The reality she was going to have to be intimate with Peter was oddly both disturbing and exciting. It felt like a betrayal of everything she and George shared. Although, she reminded herself, she was honouring his last wishes, honouring the promise she made to him.

Peter's letters arrived at regular intervals, the post seeming to be more expedient since the hostilities ended.

February 14, 1919

Happy Valentine's Day, Annie!

Tomorrow morning we sail for home on His Majesty's Troopship Canada. We're a sorry lot, I'm afraid, but so happy to be coming home to you. No time to write more. Don't try to write back as it may well be lost and never reach me. I shall be home soon. How wonderful that sounds. Home.

Spr Peter Richardson

788629

C.R.T. Depot

March 17, 1919
Ottawa, Ontario
Dear Annie,

It's official. I have my discharge papers and have been demobilized. We left Liverpool on February 15 of this year. How odd it seemed to be setting sail from that port again. But this time I have you to look forward to and not some unknown future with people I didn't know. The HMT Canada arrived in Halifax on February 23rd. From there we were loaded on a train, which was pretty crowded but all the lads were in good form, glad to be on Canadian soil at last. I'm currently in Ottawa, so not all that far from you.

Much as I would like to come straight to you, I have no money to speak of, the army is withholding my pay still. My mate, Alex is from New Westminster, BC and his father has offered to front me the money for a train ticket. As I said in a previous letter, I have a job promised peeling logs for Fraser's Mills. I can't in all good faith expect you to marry me when I have no means of supporting you. Nor I expect will your father be willing to allow such a thing when I have such bleak prospects. I hope you understand and are willing to be patient. The train leaves this afternoon. The sooner I leave the sooner I can save money to return to you. The address you can reach me at is below.

All my fondest wishes,
Peter
Contact Information
Peter Richardson
c/o Alex Franklin
327 Pine Street
New Westminster, British Columbia.

April 30, 1919
Dear Peter,

I'm sorry there wasn't time for us to meet face to face before you left for the west. I do understand your feelings in wanting to be able to provide for us, but I need you to know I have a small nest egg put away. It's not a great deal, only $100.00. I trust Father's letter has reached you by now and you are aware he has agreed to our marriage. I have some good news, Father has agreed to deed us 20 acres of his homestead. We can build a small cabin on the piece of land across the lane leading down to Doe Lake. There are good stands of timber and Ivan is helping me clear what will be the front fields looking down toward the water. It's hard work and the black flies will be swarming in the next few weeks as the weather warms, but I think of you and the life we are planning and that keeps me going.

I have some happy news. Evan and Frances were married in a quiet ceremony a few weeks ago. Frances not wanting a large affair, Father married them in the parlour with just close family and a few friends. They seem happy.

I have to confess, I miss George, as I'm sure you do as well. I feel what we are doing and the life we are planning is honouring his memory.

Your Friend
Annie

May 31, 1919
Dearest Annie,

I received your last letter with gladness. I miss George as well, more than I can ever say. It helps ease my heart to know I can care for you in his place. I confess, that is not the only reason, as I hold you in great regard for your own self and can only hope you will come to feel the same affection for me with time.

The news of your Father's generous gift of land is most welcome. Please don't over task yourself with clearing the bush. I am hopeful that by fall, or next spring at the latest I will be able to quit the mills and return to Ontario. It is growing late here and morning comes early. I had a slip with the draw knife yesterday and gave myself a good cut on the knee. Alex took a dunk in the river last week, he works unplugging the log jams which occur when they float the timber down the Fraser.

Please give my best to your brother and his new bride.

Good night for now, dear Annie.

Your Good Friend
Peter

June 26, 1919
Dear Peter,

I hope you are well healed from your mishap now and that you have managed not to sustain any other injuries. The weather here is hot and humid, the worst of the blackflies have died off, although in the bush they still seem to thrive. Now the mosquitoes are out in force. I have managed to clear an acre of land, the soil is good and should be fairly easy to plow.

I know what you mean, the day ends late and starts early. I am writing this in my room by moonlight, not wanting to waste lamp oil.

Hoping you are well and will be able to join me soon. There is a train station in Sprucedale. I checked with Chet at the station in the village. You will have to change when you get to Union Station in Toronto and then wend your way north to Sprucedale. Once you know when you will come, I will arrange to meet you in the village with the buckboard.

Your Friend

Annie

July 31, 1919
Dearest Annie,

I have great good news. I have received a bonus for my work. Alex's father may have had a hand in it as I fished Alex out of the river and saved his life after he fell between some logs when the jam broke. I happened to be down by river and heard him yell. It was a close call, for both of us, but I managed to get him out only a little battered about. He has a nasty gash on his head and was out cold when I reached him. I'm not afraid to confess it was terrifying being in the water with those huge logs shifting and banging on every side.

But the good news is I have bought a train ticket for 10 September. I'm coming to Ontario! Also, please expect to receive a package from me in the mail. I posted it two days ago, so it might even have arrived before this letter. I charge you to open it and examine the contents carefully. I trust you will be pleased with what you find.

Looking forward to seeing you very soon,
Your Good Friend,
Peter.

Chapter Seventeen

A package? I wonder what on earth Peter is sending? Annie pondered the question all the way into Sprucedale. Peter's last letter arrived twos week ago, but still no package. Today was Annie's turn to collect the mail, deliver the cream for Eaton's and pick up sundries at Mulligan's. She stopped at the train first and exchanged the cream cans, then hastened to the General Store.

"Good Afternoon, Annie," Mrs. Mulligan greeted her from behind the wide counter.

"Afternoon, Mrs. Mulligan." Annie crossed the hardwood floor, inhaling the scent of tea leaves overlaid with the sharp smell of hemp rope. Barrels of pickles stood by the counter adding their briny over notes. She handed over the list of supplies and contemplated the penny candy in the clear glass jars lining the counter top.

"I'll just get this together for you, then. Oh, by the way, I have lots of mail for you today." She winked. "A nice big parcel addressed to you, with a return address of British Columbia." Mrs. Mulligan bustled off leaving Annie to hide her burning face.

She felt somehow exposed and vulnerable to have everyone aware she was receiving parcels from a young man. Even though the whole village knew she was promised to Peter Richardson, thanks to Della. Annie decided she'd stop and see how Frances and Evan were getting on, now they were married. She missed her brother around the house since he took a job guiding summer tourists and hunters in the fall. His friend Tommy Thompson got him interested in the idea and it gave him a chance to be in the bush. He still found time to help out at the farm when needed, but on the whole he seemed much happier now.

"Here we are." Mrs. Mulligan bustled out of the back room with Annie's purchases in a sack. "Just a moment and I'll get your mail."

"Thanks. When you get a minute can I please get some licorice whips and four sour fruit balls? I'm going to stop by and see Frances and she's got quite the craving for those sour balls." Annie joined Mrs. Mulligan's giggles.

"A woman expecting a baby does have some odd notions of what tastes good. Me, I could have eaten that whole barrel of pickles when I was carrying Jake." She shook her head. "Here you are, and here's your package." Mrs. Mulligan set the mail on the counter with the sack of sundries and counted out the sweeties Annie asked for.

"Thanks. I expect Frances will have some help with the sour balls. Della has a weakness for them as well, and her not expecting at all."

Annie ran a hand over the brown paper covering the mysterious package. Little thrills ran from her fingertips to her toes with the knowledge Peter's hands wrapped the paper and tied it with twine. It made him feel nearer and more real.

After a short but happy visit with Frances and Della Annie took her leave. Returning home, she put the cream cans in the milk house and carried the rest of the things into the kitchen. After she put the sundries away, she took the brown paper wrapped package from the counter and set it on the table. Mother must be upstairs napping; she could hear the shuffle of paper from Father's study and the ring of the ax from outside where Ivan must be splitting wood by the wood shed.

She ran her hands over the paper, suddenly unwilling to open it. The anticipation was almost better than discovering the surprise. Whatever could Peter have hidden inside? Her fingers toyed with the twine, caressing the knots. Finally, she could stand the suspense no longer, and if she didn't hurry someone was sure to come in and Annie dearly wanted to open the parcel on her own.

Getting to her feet, she fetched the shears from the kitchen drawer and slid the blades over the twine. It fell loose and the paper crackled softly as it relaxed. Annie hesitated and closed her eyes taking a moment to still the rapid beat of her heart. The wrapping rattled against her trembling fingers while she folded it back to reveal a box of chocolates. Chocolates? Well, it was a nice thought...Wait, didn't the letter say to look inside carefully?

Annie picked off the cellophane wrapper and lifted the lid. Sure enough, chocolates nestled in crinkled paper in little indentations in a tray. Curious, she took each one out and lined them up before her. Nothing out of the ordinary. Her arm knocked against the empty box bottom when she reached to start replacing the candy. Ivan would enjoy the treat, and she'd share with Della as well. Something rattled under the inset tray and renewed her curiosity. What on earth... She plucked the empty tray from the box and set it aside. In the bottom of the box was a small bit of tissue. Annie picked it up and unwrapped it. A small gold ring with a tiny sapphire dropped into the palm of her hand. Tears clouded her vision and her breath caught in her throat.

Laughter bubbled in her chest. How silly and how wonderful to send her engagement ring concealed in a box of chocolates. Only Peter would think of that. How she wished he were with her so they could enjoy the moment together. But in another month he would be there. Annie closed her hand over the ring and pressed it to her heart.

"Oh George," she whispered. "I promise I'll be good to him. I promise I'll take care of him." A wisp of a breeze caressed her cheek and she leaned toward the sensation. "Go gently, my love. Til we meet again." She jumped in her chair at the sound of a door closing somewhere outside. Now who could that be? Annie put the ring in her skirt pocket and went to investigate. Her search turned up nothing and she paused in the front hall. Ivan must have left the door ajar and the wind blew it closed. That must what it was. She raised a hand to cheek.

Dipping her hand in her pocket she pulled out the ring and slid it onto the fourth finger of her left hand, turning it back and forth so the tiny gem glittered in the sunlight. Wait til Della sees this! Oh, and I suppose I must tell Father. He'll be pleased I've reconciled myself to my fate. She giggled at the thought. Suddenly the idea of spending the rest of her life with Peter didn't seem so bleak. She was fond of him after all, and she'd known him forever. He'd be changed by his experiences overseas, she supposed, but he'd still be Peter, just like Evan was still Evan.

* * *

Father and Mother were pleased with the arrival of the engagement ring. Her mother expressed the wish that it was a diamond and a wee bit bigger, but Father hushed her, much to Annie's surprise. Father, Evan, and Ivan set to work with a vengeance felling trees and dressing them in readiness to raise the walls of the small cabin on the land across the lane. There was two and a half acres cleared at the front and an area cleared against the shoulder of the big hill at the back where the barn would go. Annie was pleased with the location of the cabin. It sat at the edge of a granite outcrop that curved smooth and pleasing in front of where the front porch would be. The cabin would be high enough to never flood in the spring rains and the stone would hold the sun's heat.

She paced off the spot for the pig pen and chicken house, adding chicken wire to the list of supplies she was compiling in her head. The bottom row of logs for the cabin was in place now, and Evan was busy notching the next level of logs. How wonderful it would be if the place was at least livable by the time Peter arrived. On impulse, she spun around in the long grass by the barn clearing throwing her head back and laughing. It was going to be alright, it was going to wonderful to be the master of her own kitchen. Her own house, hers and her husband. She rather liked the idea of that now she was accustomed to thinking of Peter as her husband.

There was a loft planned where the children would sleep once they were old enough to manage the ladder. Children, maybe two boys and two girls? Annie hugged herself, it didn't really matter as long as they were healthy.

By the time August slid into September the cabin walls were up and the roof almost covered with cedar shakes. Annie loved how they rattled in the wind that swooped through the spruce trees, almost like they were sharing secrets with her. The loft was in place, but no furniture up there yet. That could wait. She took a broom and swept the wide maple planks of the floor, moving the table Ivan made for her and the two chairs. Once the roof was waterproof Della had promised to come and help carry the linens and other household things over and help set up house with her.

Annie wanted everything to be in place by the time Peter arrived sometime around the 14th or 15th of September. The wedding date was set for September 30th, although Peter didn't know that yet. Annie wrote to him after finding the ring but wasn't sure if the letter arrived before he left as she hadn't had word. She wasn't overly worried he'd object to the plans, after all it seemed he was eager as she was to start their life together. Leaning on her broom she stood in the middle of the square room imagining the colourful cloth on the table and the pine bedstead covered with the feather tick she's collected goose down for and stuffed herself, along with two pillows. She had four sets of sheets, two linen and two flannel for winter, along with a quilt made from worn out dresses and tablecloths.

She'd settled on a log cabin design rather than the double wedding ring she'd originally envisioned. The material to hand lent itself more to the former design than the latter. She smiled, no matter, there was plenty of time to make more quilts in the long winter months ahead. A small spinning wheel stood in a corner by the bed. She would use the loom up at the big house for now, the cabin just wasn't big enough, but once Peter was here they could think about adding on a room come spring.

Curtains hung at the window looking out onto the wide front porch with a view over the cleared fields to the lake. The pottery plates on the shelf gleamed, a present from her Finnish friends down at the cottages on the lake. They were almost more excited than she was about the wedding and were planning all kinds of foods for the wedding feast. Mother insisted on roasting a haunch of beef. She grinned at her mother's horror of Ana's insistence on the Finnish custom of the mother-in-law of the bride balancing a plate on her head when the couple began their first dance. When the plate fell and broke the number of pieces was supposed to foretell the number of children for the couple. Since Peter's mother was dead, Ana volunteered to act as God-mother. Ella Baldwin blanched at the thought and had left muttering about pagan heathens. Ana laughed as the custom was neither pagan nor heathen and insisted she would stand in for Peter's mother. Annie thought it was a lovely idea.

The names of some of the wedding dishes made her head spin until Ana and her friends explained what they contained in terms she could understand. They settled on Omenspirakka which was apple pie in English and Mustikkapiirake (blueberry pie) for desert. Main dishes were Lihapullat (meat balls), Kaalikaaryleet (cabbage rolls), Hernekeitto (pea soup), Rosollii (Beet root salad) and Perunarieska (potato flat bread). There was also Yorkshire pudding and mashed potatoes, turnips, beans and peas and carrots in keeping with Peter's British heritage. Evan and Tommy Thompson had promised to supply venison or maybe moose depending on what crossed their path. A haunch of beef was also earmarked for the big day. Annie was glad she didn't have to worry about the preparation of all that food on her wedding day.

There were things that could be done ahead of time which she was happy to help with, but on the big day she was excused from menial chores, thank goodness.

The days to the time of Peter's arrival alternatively seemed to both drag and fly by. Annie was busy from before daybreak until after dusk. The barn was taking shape, the pig house and chicken house were finished and waiting for their occupants who would arrive either just before or on the wedding day. Sometimes Annie thought she'd burst with excitement and happiness. If only Peter were here already. She hoped he'd approved of everything.

Chapter Eighteen

September 15th 1919 dawned in a glory of pink, cream and golden-orange clouds. Annie hitched Elsie to the buckboard, hardly able to contain her excitement. Yesterday's train came and went with no sign of Peter. He just had to be on today's train, she just knew it. Leaving Elsie tied to the gatepost with a feedbag over her ears; Annie milked the cows and gathered the eggs. She paused to admire the way the first brilliant rays of the rising sun picked out the fall colours of the trees by the cabin over the lane. Her cabin, she smiled. The roof of the small building steamed slightly as the sun burned off the thin layer of frost. Jack Frost had certainly had his paint box out recently, touching the leaves with gold and red, the rich green of the conifers seeming even deeper in comparison. How could Peter not love this place?

Leaving the milk for Ivan to separate, she placed the wicker basket of eggs by the kitchen sink and hurried upstairs to tidy her hair and give her face and hands a lick and a promise. Her stomach turned over with excitement and apprehension. She let her fingers trace the contours of her face. Have I changed much since I saw him last? What if he thinks I look old, or too fat, or to thin? Oh dear, I'm at sixes and sevens. I must get a hold of myself before I see him. How much has Peter changed? What if I don't recognize him? My stars, how embarrassing would that be?

"Quit being such a silly goose," she told her reflection. "Don't go borrowing trouble. Everything is going to be fine." Annie patted her hair into place and smoothed her skirts.

She clattered down the stairs and paused long enough to poke her head into Father's study. "I'm off to the station, Father."

He looked up from the ledger he was working on, pen in hand. "Run along then, dear. Bring your young man in as soon as you get back, Mother will have tea and sandwiches ready so we can get better acquainted with your intended."

Annie gaped at him. "Better acquainted? Why you've known Peter and his brother for years."

"That may be true, but at the time I never imagined either of those boys would be claiming your hand in marriage. There are things that need to be said."

She frowned. "Just see that you're nice about it. I'm not about to change my mind at this late date."

"Nor do I expect you to, Annabelle. Allow me my foibles, you are my youngest daughter you know, and the last daughter of this house to be married."

"Alright. We'll be sure to come directly back from the train. I do hope Peter is on today's train." She stepped out of the study door and took the front steps in a single jump. At the barn gate she removed Elsie's feed bag and hung it on the post to take back to the barn when she returned. With a light heart she stepped up on the wheel hub and gathered the lines as she settled on the wide board seat.

"Giddup there, mare," she chirped to the palomino and they set off down the sandy land at a jog the wagon rattling over the bumps. The drive through the early autumn woods was one Annie usually enjoyed, stopping often to admire Jack Frost's brush strokes in spite of her impatience. The maples were beginning to blaze with orange and red, the tamarack needles tinging with yellow, scarlet branches of the osier bushes lending colour amongst the ruddy gold-green of the berry brambles crowding the sides of the road. But today there was no dallying; the cool edge of the morning wind sent a fierce wildness galloping through her. It was all Annie could do not to whoop out loud, it felt like her blood was singing some mad song thrumming through her body.

The drive took considerably less time without pausing to listen to the birds or the wind in the tall trees. When Annie pulled up at the train depot the engine hadn't yet put in an appearance. The fall rains hadn't come yet and the bush was dry. It was a blessing the engineer hadn't had to sound his whistle to alert the local guides and inhabitants of a bush fire. It was the railway's duty to sound the alert if the train passed near a bush fire, the whistle being blasted three times twice in a row.

Annie pushed her sleeve back and consulted the watch George had sent her. The mother of pearl gleamed in the sunlight. She really was early! Leaving Elsie tied to the hitching rail; the young woman gathered the skirts of her good dress and jumped down, landing in a puff of dust. Shaking her clothes into order she set off for Mulligan's General Store. Might as well collect what mail there was, today wasn't an Eaton's cream day so she didn't have to bother with hefting heavy cans. No doubt the train would bring more mail but it would take time to sort it…But maybe it might be good to take Peter to meet Della if he wasn't too tired from his journey. Suddenly Annie was reluctant to be alone with him. Silly, she realized, but still…so much time had passed and if Evan and some of the other returning boys were anything to go by, war changed a man. Sometimes beyond recognition. Her thoughts jumped to the Bartlett boy who refused to speak to anyone and spent most of his time out in the bush, sometimes guiding silently with Tommy Thompson, or more often just off on his own. His chest was weak owing to being exposed to mustard gas more than a few times, and his face was horribly scarred by an exploding shell full of shrapnel which detonated further down the trench he was sleeping in. Annie shivered at the thought of being woken up by screams to find blood blinding you and unable to hear because of the ringing in your ears. The thoughts did nothing to ease her worry over Peter's state of mind. However, he sounded like the same old Peter in his letters, she clung to that thought.

She collected the letters and Father's newspapers along with a pound of sugar and another of loose India tea. Carry her parcels back to the buckboard she stowed them under the seat. The earth trembled under her feet and she turned to look down the track where the engine would appear coming around the big curve. Sure enough the puffing of the steam engine reached her just before the shriek of the whistle split the quiet of the morning. The sound sent the station hands springing into action, readying the small platform for the few passengers in the Pullman car, in the summer there was often a gaggle of school girls headed for Fannie's all girl camp on the far side of Doe Lake, but this late in the year passengers would be scarce.

Annie left Elsie and stepped up onto the platform, her boots echoing on the wide boards. Holding her breath she twisted her hands in her skirt, gaze fixed on the approaching Grand Trunk engine. She moved back a few steps as the train huffed to a halt with much hissing and release of steam bursts. Around her the men swarmed to bring trolleys for unloading goods and set up the small steps for the passengers to disembark. Waving a hand in front of face to disperse the smoke and steam, Annie moved toward the Pullman car. A breath of wind cleared the air and in that moment a man in a duncher cap with a knapsack slung over his shoulder stepped onto the platform. Is that him? I'm not sure. Shouldn't I know if it's Peter? It must be him…

The man removed the duncher and scrubbed a hand through his blonde hair before replacing the cap. Another shorter man jumped lithely out of the Pullman and surveyed the platform, legs akimbo, hat thrown back on his head.

Annie continued along the platform, jumping at the shriek of the whistle as the train prepared to move on. The boards trembled as the engine huffed and roared and began to pull out of the station. The air cleared, bird song reached her ears as the rumble of the departing train disappeared down the line. She paused, playing with the ribbons of her bonnet. The second man strode off toward the main part of the village. Annie watched him go, certain he wasn't Peter.

"Annabelle?" The blonde man took a tentative step toward her and removed his cap.

"Peter? Oh, I'm so happy you're finally here. I can hardly believe it," Annie babbled but she couldn't seem to stop the flood of words.

"Annabelle, Lord you have no idea how good it is to set eyes on you." Peter covered the distance between them in a few strides, halting awkwardly before her and then offering his hand.

She placed her hand in his big callused mitt, unsure if she should embrace him, offer him her cheek to kiss or shake his hand. Well, isn't this awkward. Not exactly how I dreamed this would go. His fingers closed around hers, squeezing tight, his gaze fixed intently on her face. Annie met his serious blue scrutiny with unwavering gaze, her heart thundering in her ears. Peter was taller than she remembered and more rugged. She supposed building bridges and setting up field hospitals and the like would account for that. Livid scars marred one cheek and his forehead, courtesy of the shrapnel bombs she expected. His appearance didn't matter all that much to her, underneath all that added muscle and scarring she could discern the same youth she knew so well. The realization brought a tremulous smile to her lips eliciting a thrill at the response on Peter's face.

She became aware of the interest of station master and the porters and flushed. Pulling her hand from his grasp, she hooked her hand through his elbow and led him toward the waiting wagon. "Whatever am I thinking keeping you standing here like this?" she said with false gaiety for the benefit of her audience of avid eavesdroppers. News of the encounter would be all over the village before the dust from the wagon wheels settled.

"I don't mind. It's just so nice to actually be here. There were times when I thought this day would never come." Peter smiled down at her.

Annie squeezed his arm. "I know how you feel. I've been so busy with preparations sometimes it has felt like I've been working in a void and you coming here was all a dream. That I'd wake one morning to find out this," she waved her free hand vaguely, "is just a fantasy."

He grinned. "I could pinch you to test if you're dreaming."

"I think not." She snorted. "I could pinch you if you like." Mischief danced in her eyes.

They halted at the wagon and Peter tossed his knapsack into the back of the buckboard.

"Is that everything? Or do we need to collect a trunk?" Annie eyed the long khaki bag.

"Nope, that's it, I'm afraid." He shrugged. "I'm afraid I'm not bringing much material wealth to this union, Annabelle. But I have a strong back and I can build things and I'm willing to work hard to provide for you. At some point I'm determined to pay your father for the land our cabin is built on."

"Don't be silly. Father gave us the land as a wedding present. There's no need to pay him back for anything." Annie let him assist her up onto the broad seat.

Peter looked up at her, his demeanour serious and determined. "There is need, Annabelle. A man has pride you know. I will pay your family back for their generosity. I need to know I've earned the roof over my head."

"If that's how you feel…" Annie frowned. "But it is a wedding gift. Let's worry about monetary things later. Today I just want to enjoy having you here."

Peter strode around, untied Elsie, and stepped up onto the seat beside her. She laid a hand on his arm as he picked up the lines.

"Turn into the village, I want you to meet my friend, Della. And maybe my brother Evan and his wife Frances if he's to home."

"If you like. Giddup, horse." He slapped the lines lightly on the palomino's rump and turned her head toward the village centre. Peter glanced at her as the mare ambled along. "How is the cabin coming along? And what still needs to be done before the wedding?"

"Oh, the cabin is ready. That's where I thought you could stay until the wedding. Unless you'd rather stay in the big house in the guest room? I just thought you might like the privacy and Rotha will arriving, and Hetty and Clarence are planning to come to stay two days beforehand and..." she broke off, unsure of his reaction.

"The cabin will be fine." He offered a reassuring smile. "After living on top of each other in the troopship and crowded on the trains, the solitude will be welcome."

"That's settled, then. Oh, just pull in here, Della's is the yellow house with the white porch." Annie pointed toward a neat house shaded by towering oaks.

The visit with Della went splendidly with Della drawing Peter out about his job in British Columbia. The conversation seemed to put him

259

more at ease, the tension easing in his body and his features. After taking leave of Della they drove by Evan and Frances' place but the couple weren't home. Annie was quiet on the drive home content to observe her future husband as he took in his surroundings.

"It's not so much different from Eganville, is it?" he commented, eyes on the mixed soft and hard wood bush crowding both sides of the sandy road.

"No, it's still Ontario bush," she agreed. "Although, the snow tends to come earlier and stay a bit later. Maybe because we're so close to Georgian Bay. We will have to borrow Father's sledge for moving snow drifts this year as I don't think we'll have time to build our own before the snow flies. Oh, did I tell you the out buildings are almost ready?"

Peter shook his head and swatted at a mosquito.

"The chicken house and pig pen are roofed and the logs chinked, so they're ready for winter. I put in a false floor and packed the space between it and the ground with lots of straw. Ivan says it's a lot of work for nothing, but I think it will help keep them warmer. The barn is roofed and the walls chinked, the feed room is roughed in, the loft floor is done but there are no stalls yet. I wanted to wait on that anyway as I wasn't sure if you wanted straight stalls or loose boxes. What do you think?" Annie turned sideways toward him, knocking her knee against his thigh. A thrill of reaction shot through her, an answering colour stained Peter's ruddy cheeks. His gaze slid toward her, hot and bright.

"I suppose it will depend on how many head we have and what kind," Peter's voice was gravelly and he cleared his throat while pressing his leg into her knee.

"Well," she said sliding a bit closer to him, "I made enough money the last few years selling jams and jellies, along with my egg money to buy us a work horse for the fields. The Finlanders have got together and Ana told me on the sly they're planning to give us a pregnant sow. We'll need to buy a milk cow in the spring, for this winter we can take from Father's cows. I have a couple of sacks of seed potatoes and onions and some small jars of carrot, beet and cabbage seeds. I've already got vegetables and apples in our very own root cellar. I built it into the shoulder of the big hill behind the cabin. There's still lots of wood to split for the wood shed, and some late cabbage and kale to bring in. Oh, this is so exciting! Having you here makes everything so oh, I don't know…real." Annie fairly bounced on the seat with contained excitement.

"Sounds like you've got things well in hand. I'm impressed." Peter's smile was brilliant.

They rode along in silence for a bit, the sun slanting through the trees and laying bright patches across the road. Annie laid her hand on his arm, conscious of the hard slide of muscle beneath her fingers. The watch moved on her wrist reminding her of its presence. She pulled her sleeve up to expose it, suddenly shy.

"I wore your mother's watch today. The one George gave me…he said he talked it over with you…" she let the words trail off.

Peter dropped his gaze from the road, switched the lines to one hand and closed his fingers over hers. "Yes, we both wanted you to have it." His face clouded for a moment. "I just wish…"

"I know. We both wish he was here…" Annie's throat closed and choked off her words.

He pulled the wagon to a stop and hitched the lines over the brake handle. Peter turned and took both her hands in his. "Are you sorry, Annie? I mean, do you regret agreeing to marry me? I know you and George had an understanding, but I want you to know I've always been very…fond…of you. It was just, well; I knew I didn't stand a chance. What with the way the two of you looked at each other a blind man could tell how the land lay. I promise to be good to you, take care of you…and not just because I promised my brother."

Annie blinked back tears, relieved he finally called her Annie rather than Annabelle. "Oh Peter, of course I wish George was here. I hate it that he died in the stupid war. But no, I don't regret saying I'd marry you. Not at all. I can't see my life without you by my side now. I hope we have a big happy family. Oh! You do want children, right? We've never really had a chance to talk about things like that." She paused to study his expression.

"Yes, yes. I want lots of young'uns." His sudden smile was like sunlight breaking through storm clouds. "Girls who look like you and boys who take after the Richardson side of the family. Do you think we could call the first boy George?" He caught his bottom lip in his teeth.

"I'd like that," she whispered. "We'll call the first little girl after your mother. What was her name?"

"Ellen."

Annie giggled. "That's perfect. My mother is Ella, so she'll think we named her after her, and we won't disabuse her of that notion." She leaned her head against his. "I'm really happy. Are you?"

"You make me happier than I thought possible, Annie. But we'd best shake a leg or they'll be sending out a search party for us." He dared a kiss on her knuckles and placed her hands in her lap before picking up the lines. "Did the chocolates arrive safely?" he asked without looking at her.

Annie pulled off her left glove and wiggled her fingers at him. "Why yes, the chocolates arrived just fine. And look what I found in the box." Light sparked off the sapphire.

"That's a relief. I was worried something would go wrong and I was almost afraid to ask." He grinned.

"I should have told you right off, I was just so overwhelmed you were finally here I totally

263

forgot. I meant to show you when you got off the train. That was how I planned it, anyway."

"It doesn't matter now, does it? Everything's fine." Peter clucked to the mare.

"Yes, everything's just fine now you're here." Annie leaned against his shoulder while the autumn leaves showered down on them.

Chapter Nineteen

Annie was awake before the old rooster could crow. She bounced out of bed and danced around the room, stopping to poke Rotha in the shoulder where she slumbered in the cot by the wall.

"Wake up, sleepyhead! It's my wedding day. Wake up!"

Rotha rolled over, opened one eye a slit and groaned. "Saints preserve me, Annie. Go back to bed, even the chickens aren't up yet."

"Don't care! It's my wedding day, how can I think about sleeping?" She glanced over at the white gown hanging on the hook by the window; the material glowed even in the dim light. It was perfect. A nice walking length, with no train to trip over and get muddled up with. Mother insisted Annie wear the long China silk gloves that came up past her elbows. The very same gloves Mother wore when she wed Father. Both Hetty and Rotha had worn them before her. It was a shame Rotha's husband hadn't been able to make the trip, but her sister was here. Alice had sent a note from Ireland with a bit of dyed blue Irish lace inside. Her something 'blue'. Annie hugged herself.

Pulling back the curtain she looked toward the cabin across the lane. A light showed in the front window. Annie grinned. Peter couldn't sleep either. Overhead the sable velvet of the sky was starting to soften and a pearly light crept about the tops of the trees and over the lake. She knelt at the window sill and leaned her chin on her hands enjoying the gentle harbingers of the approaching dawn. The strengthening light pushed the shadows back into the bush and the cranky old rooster finally deigned to announce the imminent arrival of the day.

The day promised to one of the perfect fall days. The sun rose in golden glory turning the autumn woods into torches of colour. The air was still morning cool but promised to be pleasantly warm by the time the mist burned off the hollows. A light breeze tousled the leaves, sending a few spiralling down to the ground. No clouds marred the blue bowl of the sky; Annie opened the window and inhaled the familiar scents of forest and farm.

She turned her gaze skyward for a moment. "I know you're up there watching us, George. I wish you were here with me, but that's not what God planned for us. Please give Peter and I your blessing and watch out for us until we can be together again," Annie whispered, pressed her fingers to her lips and blew a kiss to the blue sky morning.

* * *

Once the household awoke, events moved faster than Annie would have thought possible.

266

Rotha, and even Hetty, fussed with her hair and her clothes. Hetty lent her a pair of satin dancing slippers to wear with her wedding dress with a strict injunction to make sure they didn't get dirty or come within a mile of a cow pie. Annie giggled and promised to do her best. Her hair was pulled and twisted and wound around curling irons heated in the kitchen cook stove until Annie was sure it would either catch fire or fall out altogether. She had to admit though that the person looking back at her from the mirror was beautiful, even if it didn't look her.

Ana and a few of the other Finlander ladies stopped by to wish her luck before the wedding and share some of their traditions with her. Some of them made sense and some made her giggle. Annie rather like the idea of having a canvas canopy held over the bride and groom while they took their vows. It was called a 'bridal sky' and was usually blue. Mother would have a fit if she suggested it, but it was a lovely idea.

Hetty insisted Annie eat a bit of toast and jam even though she was sure nothing would stay where she put it. "Better to try than have you passing out at the altar," her oldest sister replied tartly. "Heaven only knows what the neighbors would think."

"Oh Hetty," Rotha scolded. "They'd think she was nervous for heaven's sake. The boy hasn't been here long enough for it to be anything more scandalous than that."

"You can never be too careful of your reputation," she said in a prim voice.

Rotha rolled her eyes at Annie behind the older woman's back.

Toast and jam dispensed with, Annie let herself be herded back up the stairs to get dressed. In fact, she did little but stand there and do as she was told. She was sure she could have accomplished things in half the time if they'd just let her alone, but that had a snowball's chance in hell of happening, as Evan would say.

I hope Peter isn't getting pestered like this. I wouldn't blame him if he took to his heels and ran if he is. But he won't. I know he won't. He promised me, and he promised George. He'll be waiting for me at the altar. It was comforting to realize there was someone she could count on to be there for her, no matter what. Everything was going to be fine. Just fine.

The buzz of conversation drifted up form below in the front yard. Annie moved toward the open window to see who was there.

"Annabelle! Whatever do you think you're doing?" Hetty was appalled.

"I'm just going to see who has arrived."

"No, you most certainly are not." Hetty towed her away from the window. "What if someone sees your dress before the ceremony? Or worse, what if your husband to be sees you? That's so bad luck. You just can't chance it."

Annie sighed. "I don't understand how any of that can matter in the whole scheme of things.

But if it will keep you happy, fine. I won't look out."

"Hetty's right, Annie. Better safe than sorry, no point in tempting fate," Rotha sided with the elder sister.

"Can I sit down at least?" Annie hovered by the straight back chair near the bed.

"I suppose, but only if you're very careful," Hetty allowed.

"Good, because my feet are already hurting. How do dance in these things?" She held one leg out and twisted her foot from side to side.

"If you didn't have the feet of a man you'd have no problem. I assure you I find them quite comfortable." Hetty sniffed and looked down her nose at her sister.

"Well, I assure you, I find them quite uncomfortable. But thank you for lending them to me all the same, they do look nice with the dress." Annie sought to soothe Hetty's ruffled feathers. The last thing she needed as a set-to with her today.

Rotha disappeared and returned with a pitcher of lemonade and three glasses. "I thought we could use something to drink. The day is becoming quite warm." She set things on the small bedside table and poured three glasses. Standing in front of Annie, she raised her glass. "To Annie, may she have a long and happy marriage."

"To Annie," Hetty echoed her.

269

"Thanks," Annie said and took a sip from the glass in her hand careful not to drip on the fine linen.

The clock in the downstairs hall struck the quarter hour. Rotha went to check on the proceedings on the front lawn. "Almost time, Annie. Let's get your headdress on. I see Father headed this way."

Annie stood up, conscious of the pinch of the slippers on her toes. She stood stoic while her sisters fussed with the froth of tulle and arranged wild flowers into the head piece and her curls. Wild purple asters, a bit of goldenrod, some pansies for thoughts, late pink summer roses for joy and grace. Her bouquet lay on the chest of drawers. Also wild flowers Annie collected herself. White roses for constancy, more pink ones, a red one for love, more asters, she'd added some creamy white and cerise yarrow for their feathery fronds as well as colour. The whole was tied with cream and pink ribbons. She took a deep breath and picked up the flowers at the sound of Father's tread on the stairs.

"Are you ready, Annabelle?" He stood in the doorway. "You look lovely, my dear."

"Thank you, Father. And, yes I'm ready. I think?" She turned to consult her sisters.

"Yes, you'll do," Hetty said and waved her onward with a flap of her hand.

"You're beautiful." Rotha hugged her carefully and air kissed her cheek.

"Shall we?" Father offered her arm.

270

"Wait. Give us a chance to get down to our places," Hetty said.

Her sisters gathered their shawls and reticules and hurried down the stairs, their heels clattering on the front hall floor.

"I believe we can proceed now." Father offered his arm again.

Annie tucked her hand into his elbow and let him lead her down the stairs. They hesitated just inside the front door, Hetty gave a signal and the church organist struck up the Wedding March on the upright piano Evan, Peter and Ivan had manhandled out of the parlour and onto the wide porch earlier. Rotha nodded from her place by the side of the door and Annie stepped out of the shadows into the sunlight spilling across the porch. She almost stumbled at the murmur of appreciation that greeted her appearance. A movement at the head of the flower and leaf strewn aisle between the rows of chairs caught her attention.

Peter stood beside the lectern with Evan and Ivan at his side. The dark suit was obviously new, the white shirt stiff with starch, cuffs shot below the jacket sleeves. His appearance took her breath away, how handsome he was. His blonde hair shone in the light, grey eyes serious with a warm welcome lurking underneath. The strangeness she'd experienced with her first glimpse of him vanished and she smiled. Father took the first step and Annie walked gracefully at his side down the wide steps and up the grassy aisle. Della waited at the end on the bride's side as her Maid of Honour. Annie held her head high and kept her gaze trained on Peter as she drew nearer. Finally, they reached the lectern and Father placed her hand on Peter's arm.

Father insisted that no one except him could perform the ceremony even though he was also Father of the Bride. The ceremony was a blur to Annie, she supposed she must have said the right things at the appropriate time, and Peter must have done the same, because after a particularly fiery sermon full of hell fire and brimstone Peter slipped a simple gold band on her finger and Father pronounced them man and wife.

Arm in arm Annie walked beside her new husband back down the grassy path. Her lips still tingled from the wedding kiss and she found that in spite of Hetty's dour warnings she was quite looking forward to her wedding night.

As soon as politely possible, Annie discarded the fancy slippers and put them safely on top of the upright piano still installed on the porch. It would be moved back into the parlour after the supper or the damp would get into it. The big barn was cleared out and the fiddlers were already tuning their instruments accompanied by someone on the accordion and another with a harpsichord. She wriggled her cramped toes in the cool grass before pulling on her high button boots that thankfully fit correctly.

"Happy?" Peter came up behind her and slid his arms around her waist.

"Very," she said, leaning back into his solid warmth. "And you?"

"Happier than a man has right to be," he replied and pressed a kiss to the back of her neck.

Mother had tried to prepare Annie for the wedding night, but her advice was 'lay back, lift your linen and let him have his way with you'. Hetty was only slightly better; she explained the physical act with much blushing and stammering as if Annie hadn't seen animals engaged in the act. It wasn't as if she had no idea where babies came from. But no one prepared her for the sensations racing through her at Peter's touch. It was frightening, but in a very pleasurable way and not at all what her conversation with Hetty had led her to expect.

The supper was demolished and the dancing began. Annie danced til she was out of breath and her feet hurt again. She was having a grand time, but a part of her wished to escape the laughter and noise and retire to the little cabin where the quilt covered feather bed waited for them. No doubt some of the wilder participants would engage in a chivary. Hopefully Ivan, who had been sent after supper to guard the cabin and make sure no one played any tricks, had been successful and here would be no unpleasant surprises in the bed. Although, Annie remembered the huge bull frog her and Della had managed to place in Hetty and

Clarence's marriage bed. Turnabout was fair play, she supposed, but fervently wished nothing similar awaited her.

Finally, the party slowed down a bit, taking advantage of the lull, Peter and Annie slipped away. It was only a short walk from the main farm to their small cabin. Peter held her hand and steadied her over the rough ground in the dark. Annie's head was pleasantly muzzy with exhaustion. Although it was supposed to be a dry party, she was fairly sure some of the boys had secreted a few jugs of moonshine and homemade beer in the milk house. Peter however didn't smell of drink, which she was glad of.

They woke Ivan when they arrived at the cabin and sent him to join the party which would probably go on until the sun came up. Peter led her into the main room.

"Shall I light the lamp?" He hesitated with the striker in hand.

"Let's not. If there's no light maybe they'll think we're not in here." Annie fussed with removing her veil.

"Here, let me help with that." Peter's breath stirred the curls at her temples and his fingers plucked the pins and wilted flowers from her hair. At last it fell free around her shoulders, his hands running through the tangled curls. "Your hair is so soft. You know I haven't seen you with your hair down since we were kids." His eyes gleamed in the dim light.

"It feels wonderful to get all those pins out of it." She tipped her head back.

"Annie," he whispered and pulled her against him. "I know George was your first love and I can't expect you to feel the same about me. But you need to know something. I have always loved you, right from when we were kids. I hope you will come to love me in time. I'm a patient man, I can wait." He buried his face in her hair.

"Peter, I do love you. You're right, not like I loved George. But I do love you and it's enough to build our life on." She leaned back and grinned at him. "This is our wedding night and there will only be two of us in the marriage bed. That much I can promise you. Just you and me."

"You have no idea how much that means to me to hear you say that." Tears glistened in his eyes. He swept her up, dress and all, and carried her to the waiting feather bed.

Epilogue

Decades later, Annie closed Peter's eyes as he drew his last breath and kissed his lips. "Thank you for loving me," she whispered.

That night she dreamed. George walked with her on the banks of the Bonnechere River, they were young again. Hand in hand they rambled over their childhood haunts. In the green wood under the boughs of the blooming apple trees with trout lilies around their feet, he took her face in his hands and kissed her as he never had the chance to in life.

"Thank you for taking such care of my brother, Annie. I'll be waiting for you as I've waited all these years for my brother's bride."

Bibliography

Journals of Capel Baldwin St. George
The years 1911 - 1920

Doctor Barnardo Homes
Canadianhomechildren.weebly.com/indentu
redservants.html
Winnipegfreepress.com/special/ourcityyour
world/uk/thebarnardoboys-149343895.html
Torontoist.com/2014/08/historicist-dr-
barnardos-children
Pier21.ca/wp-content/uploads/filesFirst_75-
years/research_home_children.pdf

World War 1
http://cefresearch.ca/wiki/index.php/Troops
hips:_Repatriation
http://www.firstworldwar.com/source/armis
ticeterms.htm
http://www.bac-
lac.gc.ca/eng/discover/military-
heritage/first-world-war/personnel-
records/Pages/personnel-records.aspx
http://cmhs.ca/index.php/menu-l-articles/2-
uncategorised/19-cmhs-article-abbreviations#D
https://www.thestar.com/news/walking_the
_western_front/2014/05/walking_the_weste
rn_

front__where_the_tanks_rumbled_before_d
awn_.html
https://www.theguardian.com/education/20
14/jul/23/first-world-war-slang-glossary

Ontario in early 1900's
https://ttlastspring.com/2016/05/
http://www.exporail.org/can_rail/Canadian
%20Rail_no156_1964.pdf
Google Earth for Southern Ontario Railway
Maps
http://images.techno-
science.ca/?en/stories/train_journey/d/page/1
http://www.proto87.org/ca/history/Pembrok
eSouthernRy.html
https://www.pinterest.com/pin/3404440530
65270657/
https://www.google.ca/maps/place/Eganvill
e,+ON/@45.5343291,7.1148353,14z/data=
!3m1!4b1!4m5!3m4!1s0x4cd15eb9c217e49
b:0xa574225b8c153200!8m2!3d45.539935!
4d-77.1010788
http://www.bonnecherecaves.com/
https://en.wikipedia.org/wiki/Ottawa,_Arnp
rior_and_Parry_Sound_Railway
http://www.ghosttownpix.com/ontario/intro
s/scotia.html
http://www.thecanadianencyclopedia.ca/en/
article/grand-trunk-railway-of-canada/
https://www.collectionscanada.gc.ca/confed
eration/023001-3010.25-e.html

More Books by this author from
Books We Love
Canadian Historical Brides Series
His Brother's Bride ~ Ontario

The Cornwall Adventures
Laurel's Quest ~ Book One
A Step Beyond ~ Book Two
Go Gently ~ Book Three
Romance
Storm's Refuge A Longview Romance Book
One
Come Hell or High Water A Longview
Romance Book Two
A Longview Wedding
A Longview Christmas Seasonal Novella

Arabella's Secret Series
The Selkie's Song ~ Book One
Arabella Dreams ~ Book Two
Co-Authored with Pat Dale
The Last Cowboy
Henrietta's Heart
The Teddy Dialogues

Historical Horror
By N.M. Bell
No Absolution

Nancy M Bell has publishing credits in poetry, fiction and non-fiction. Nancy has presented at the Surrey International Writers Conference and the Writers Guild of Alberta Conference. She loves writing fiction and poetry and following wherever her muse takes her.

Please visit her webpage
http://www.nancymbell.ca
She posts on the Books We Love Blog on the 18th of every month
http://bwlauthors.blogspot.ca/

You can find her on Facebook at
http://facebook.com/NancyMBell
Follow on twitter: @emilypikkasso

bookswelove.com

Made in the USA
Monee, IL
09 December 2022

19946418R00155